THE FLAT AND WEIGHTLESS TANG-FILLED FUTURE & OTHER STORIES

LYN FAIRCHILD HAWKS

Second Print Edition: June 2013
First Print Edition: January 2013

ISBN-10: 0-9888837-4-0
ISBN-13: 978-0-9888837-4-1

Print Formatting: Streetlight Graphics

"Midrift" was first published in 2008 in *Relief* Journal Volume 2.3.

To Doris, who said I should keep writing.

TABLE OF CONTENTS

ACKNOWLEDGMENTS

I'm grateful for the love and support of my parents, Katherine and Steve, and for my sister, Antonia, who sees promise in everything I write. Amy and Carolina have always been there for me, reminding me to never apologize for my passion. I'm thankful for the careful, keen eye of Bob, my Peaceniks colleague, who's cheered me and my stories on for quite some time. I'm blessed to have the perspective of fellow writers—Gordon, Jennifer, Stephanie, Delia, Dave, Nancy, and Ruth, who give inspiration and careful, insightful critiques of my work. I am also fed by the gathering of wonderful women—Marcia, Beverly, Laurie, Susan, and Katie—where some of these stories were born.

Thanks to Diane who provided a careful review of this manuscript, catching all those grammar and mechanics things an English teacher oughta know but somehow forgets when it's her own writing.

Relief Journal, the AROHO Foundation, and the NCSU, Glimmer Train, and Writers' Group of the Triad contests have recognized my stories, helping me keep the faith to stay with this crazy writing thing. The North Carolina Writers' Network gifted me with an opportunity to work closely with Doris Betts through the Elizabeth Daniels Squire Residency, and it was a turning point in my life to think my second career might be my childhood dream-author.

My husband Greg always understands this hunger to put words on a page. Thank you, my love, for sharing the artist's way with me.

BY THE WATER

THE MAN KEPT A GRIP on the hands of his youngest one and his middle one, and told the oldest to stay close as the four stumbled down the hot, soft sand to the water. How he hated grit rasping between his toes, the E. coli waiting in the waves, and the violent shrieks of gulls and beachgoers. But it was a rare weekend with the boys and he was not to be outdone by Marjorie and her elaborate, overscheduled hoopla as custodial parent.

In the shallows, the water swirled gray green, full of sediment and pocked with soapy foam. Farther out, pelicans floated like fat black cats on the waves, the sight of them making the youngest point and squeal. The man told his sons to wait and let water lap around their ankles because their body temperatures needed to acclimate. It was the warmest water he had ever felt—in the seventies—but he had to buy some time while his mind scrambled and heart raced. Supervising a four-, eight-, and twelve-year-old simultaneously on miles of beach: an impossible proposition.

He looked north and south, yet saw no one else saddled with three children, and boys at that. To his right, there was a little girl supervised by her obese mother, who was in turn aided by *her* obese mother. Between them, enough buoyancy to support the entire crew of an oil rig. To his left, a white-trash guy complete with a box goatee and Jesus-wrestling-a-devil tattoo, looming over his only charge, a chubby toddler, while his wife snapped pictures of Baby's First Swim with a camera too expensive to be anything but stolen. A two-to-one ratio, everywhere. The unbalanced proportions of his group squeezed him into a dangerous predicament where jagged shells, slimy seaweed, and unknown creatures of the *Jaws*-filled deep surged close, while the example of thrill-seeking fools egged his sons farther out. When he was eighteen, he had never dreamed of life formulas rendering outputs like this. Yet here he was—caged.

The oldest, who insisted on being called "J" though his name was Jeremiah, watched him resentfully, perhaps because their party lacked what others boasted: raft, floaties, foam tubing, boogie boards. The youngest, Bobby, hung from his father's hand like a dead weight, twisting, turning, squealing, "Daddy, Daddy! Make me swim!" The middle, Stephen Alex, stood like a statue, his hand limp like soft bread in his father's grip, eyes fixed on something beyond the pelicans.

Marjorie, of course, would shame him when she took the boys here later this summer: thanks to alimony and child support, she could haul an obscene amount of toys plus a nanny.

He felt a wave of burn wash through his lungs. He said, "Everyone back to the tent."

"What?" cried Jeremiah.

"Back to the tent. You can't all swim at once."

"Unbelievable, Martin," Jeremiah said under his breath.

"Believe it," Martin snapped. "You want the deaths of your brothers on your head?"

Bobby screamed, "Me first! Me, me, me!"

"Tent first, check sunscreen, then you and I'll go back out."

He liked returning to the massive gazebo with a shade area one hundred feet square. No one within five hundred yards had anything like it. The fabric provided 90 percent UV block and reduced the ambient air temperature below it up to 33 percent.

Jeremiah threw himself down on the blanket, his face dark with anger. Bobby hopped on each foot, scattering sand on clean towels, knocking totes over. Stephen Alex, who knew the tent measurements by heart and served as Martin's right-hand man during assembly, squatted on his haunches and watched something invisible out on the water.

"Don't move," Martin said to the other two. He grabbed Bobby's hand and left for the water.

Entertaining a four-year-old was easy. The boy was content to cling to Martin and find treasure in the wet sand where water was only a few inches deep. Bobby squealed if the water nipped at his ankles, and he marveled at the pulsing holes, leaking sand and bubbles, where the tiny crabs hid. He yelled and pointed when minnows glided by in the shallows; he cackled at the swooping gulls screeching over bread tossed by a brainless teen girl. Martin found himself smiling. This was parenting; this he could do. Whenever he looked back, he saw his other two sitting like stones beneath the huge, impressive tent.

Jeremiah was next because Stephen Alex said he didn't mind waiting, and Martin knew this was not a lie. The boy had no doubt exhausted himself swimming laps at the pool this morning while Martin sat nearby with an espresso, the other two asleep back at the condo. That one was just like him at age eight, driven with a secret mission, whether the tallest Lego tower or twenty laps in ten minutes. A solo player, that one: quiet and always in his own head. Stephen Alex had eyes gray as rock and just as impenetrable.

Jeremiah wanted to swim beyond the crashing waves: not an option with two more to watch and Stephen Alex often spacing out. The boy ducked as water hit his face, then sneaked out some more. "You're waist deep," Martin called. "Stay there and do laps."

"I want to swim out there," Jeremiah yelled, looking toward the horizon.

"Swim here."

"You're so lame."

Martin was pretty sure the fool with the goatee heard that, and worse, winked at him, like they were two putzes together in this rollicking game of parenting.

Martin called, "So you want to lose a little brother? What if you swim that far, I have to turn my back, and they wander off and drown?"

The obese grandmother glanced up from her beached-whale sprawl while the gritty toddler climbed all over her. Jeremiah flushed pink. Martin yelled, louder, "The pool is cleaner. We're going there later."

Jeremiah turned away, waves surging around him, somehow maintaining balance in the onslaught. He was nothing but bone and stringy muscle with a concave bird chest and E.T.-like appendages. He seemed ridiculous, as all pre-teen boys did, but especially when he argued, looking like a skeleton gathering nonexistent muscle for a fight. Marjorie claimed Martin "alienated" Jeremiah and needed to "talk to him like he's a young man." What did she know about being a boy or a man? About the financial demands a family made? Her jobs consisted of PTA this and volunteer that. She'd never drawn more than an occasional paycheck in her life, except at the crafts store where she was working when he met her. At first she was happy to spend her time taking care of him, cooking and improving the home, until Jeremiah came, and then the other two, all of whom she indulged to excess while ignoring the one who kept everything afloat. Now she bought Jeremiah every tech toy on first release, whatever was most needless and far beyond his age: last month, a Droid phone and iPod, after a year of Xbox, Guitar Hero, and Modern Warfare. The boy had soft hands, a soft brain, and no idea what work was.

Jeremiah yelled, "Why are we even out here?"

Martin couldn't respond because Bobby came charging down the beach, hell bent for the water.

Back at their rented condo, the mirror showed how the sun had blasted his skin, despite the SPF 50 and zinc oxide. Lotion settled into cracks around his eyes as if his whole face might be turning to limestone. He hated Marjorie for stealing his best years.

The boys gobbled their bologna sandwiches, Doritos, and Mountain Dew in five minutes, and then Bobby dashed to the door, screaming, "Pool!" Why the boys wouldn't nap or even consider an hour in front of the TV was beyond him. Bobby's frantic energy propelled all of them like a bush-league basketball team up and down the court of vacation till their tongues hung out. Marjorie, to her credit, could somehow march them everywhere at double time, never tiring, always delighting them with something new and enthralling. For a few seconds, he actually missed her efficiency and energy. One thing the woman was not: lazy.

Bobby squealed like a swine all the way down the outdoor stairs till Jeremiah cuffed him on the head. Bobby was too excited to cry. At the pool cabana they could access the floaties, rafts, and every toy to spoil a child. As they came through the gate into the pool area, Martin saw only one woman sunbathing there; other families had the good sense to nap during the most intense sun of the day.

At least sixty, the woman was brown as burnt toast, with

5

gold lipstick, a halo of frizzed white hair, and oversized sunglasses. She gave Martin a fake smile of white, white teeth that looked like someone else had donated her a mouth. Then she turned back to the book she clutched, a thick Danielle Steel hardback. Good. Like him, she wanted to be left alone.

"Get in the pool," he ordered. "Shallow end for you, buddy," he said to Bobby. "And stay with your brother." He pointed to Stephen Alex. Best not to assign Bobby to Jeremiah, who with that nasty scowl needed to dive deep and not resurface for a while.

Stephen Alex helped Bobby onto a raft and began pushing him around the pool. Bobby called, "Look, Dad! I'm the captain!" and then started a putt-putt spitting sound that fortunately didn't carry like the squeals.

Martin perched on the edge of a bleached, sagging chaise lounge. He leaned on his knees, staring at the chlorinated water. Despite another application of sunscreen, he could feel the sun sealing his fate. He pictured melanoma sprouting on his nose, his receding hairline, his shins, all exposed parts. Damn it, he'd left his hat behind in the frenzy to get out of the condo. He smelled rank as the sea.

"Cute boys," the woman called. She was reclined three chaises over, close enough that beneath the dark tan he saw thighs riddled with cellulite, and beneath the satin-white bathing suit, long and useless breasts. She had a ravenous look, demanding conversation. He'd misread that smile. If only faces came with subtitles.

"They should be napping," Martin said.

"Boys will be boys."

"Especially when they're spoiled."

That shut her up for a moment. He enjoyed the brief peace.

"You don't seem the type to spoil."

"No."

"So you're solo parenting?"

"Yes."

"Just for today?"

"The weekend."

"Where's your wife?"

"My ex? She's at a scrapbooking conference."

The woman's lip curled. "No wonder you divorced her."

Martin glanced at her, startled. Then he said carefully, because he could see Jeremiah craning his neck from the deep end to hear, "There were many reasons. I'm sure she could give you a list."

In fact, a scrapbooked one. Their fifteen years of marriage had produced one other tangible besides the boys: a library full of Blessed Memories—glossy, die-cut, embellished shots captioned by vellum strips of scripture. From birth those boys had been stars of her slick albums.

The woman smiled. "Oh, no doubt. Women are good at honey-do and honey-don't."

He cracked a smile. It felt strange—stiff and sore in his cheeks. Then he heard Jeremiah taunting Stephen Alex: "You're so slow, you'll never do a mile. Bobby weighs like two pounds. Like that's going to train you?"

"Three boys. That's a lot." This woman was determined to make him talk.

"Yes. A handful." Then before he could stop himself: "Except that one. He's quiet, thank God."

The woman peered over her fly eyeballs at Stephen Alex who, silent as a shark, paddled a steady stream behind Bobby—pushing, pushing, pushing.

"Five!" Bobby shouted. "Go, Stevie, go!"

"It's taking you like *forever*," Jeremiah crowed.

Stephen Alex smiled but said nothing.

"Still waters," she said.

That was exactly what Martin's grandmother had said of Martin when he was a boy, the expression always followed by a fierce hug. She was the only one he never shook off. Large like a cow, she had a warm, slow safeness about her that calmed Martin's frequent panic attacks. She taught him words like *please* and *thank you*, words she said were necessary if you didn't want people thinking you were a potted plant.

"This is boring," Jeremiah yelled. "Let's go."

Martin looked at the woman, who winked at him.

"Your attitude is boring," Martin said.

Jeremiah's face turned red under the woman's gaze.

She chuckled. "How old is he, fifteen?"

"No, almost thirteen."

"Tall for his age."

Martin nodded. "The oldest and youngest are in the ninety-ninth percentile." Unfortunately, Stephen Alex was looking to be a runt. In that way and in that way only, he took after Marjorie.

"So what am I supposed to *do*?" Jeremiah screamed.

It was so loud, everyone twitched.

"Do?" snapped Martin. "Swim, you idiot. You sure aren't impressing me or the lady here." He had twice used this line with some success in restaurants, now that Jeremiah was showing occasional interest in girls.

Jeremiah yelled, "*Lady?* Where?"

Martin looked at the woman. Her smile grew tight as if someone had shellacked her face. It had to be big, his action. He yelled, "Get out of the pool, now!"

He strode over to where Jeremiah clung to the side of the deep end, grabbed his arm, and yanked him up. The boy scraped his arm along the concrete and fell on his stomach.

Martin bellowed, "Now get up!"

Tears clung to Jeremiah's lashes, but he refused to cry. He stumbled to his feet. Behind them, Martin heard Bobby's whimpers and Stephen Alex speaking quietly to him.

Martin threw a towel at Jeremiah and said to the other two, "Get out." Then to Jeremiah: "Apologize to that lady. Now."

Jeremiah rubbed the towel across his bird chest, his face red and puckered. The scrape on his arm bloomed pink and speckled with blood. Head down, he walked toward the woman, stopped several feet from her, and muttered, "Sorry." He turned and came back.

"Oh, no," Martin said. "Do it again. Look her in the eye." The boy could have his same torture. The grandparents Jeremiah never had to endure used to do worse whenever Martin struggled to make eye contact. *Look them in the eye*: it was a command with such darkness at its edges, it felt like cussing when Martin said it.

Jeremiah stood still a few seconds, making Martin wonder if he would have to shove him back to the woman. She looked like someone had struck her across the face. She said quietly, "Once is enough."

"Do it," Martin snapped at Jeremiah. Then he said to her, "He needs to learn."

Jeremiah trudged up to her, kept the same distance, and raised his head like a mechanical doll. "I'm sorry," he said. Martin guessed Jeremiah was staring somewhere around the vicinity of her neck.

It would have to do.

Martin turned to the other two and said, "Your brother acted like an idiot and therefore, he gets treated like an idiot. Bobby, don't you *ever* let me catch you acting like this."

Bobby burst into high-pitched, desperate wails.

Martin led one, snot-faced and screaming, and the other two, trailing towels, away from the pool. He left without saying goodbye because something choked his throat so hard he could barely breathe.

Their mother was to blame. He knew this as he marched them back. Politeness, consideration, quiet—all foreign concepts to Marjorie, who didn't teach manners. If she had written the Bible—and no doubt she soon would craft a Blessed Memories version—the first line would be, *Thy kids are always right.* And now look at them. Monsters.

Back at the condo, he sent Jeremiah to his bedroom while he allowed the other two to watch TV. Martin told Bobby and Stephen Alex he was going to lie down and they were not to move till dinnertime.

The grating, bouncy sounds of a *Nickelodeon* show hammered his door, but once prone, he could calm his breathing and use his word. *Stay. Stay. Stay...* The word stopped the pacing and the tapping, the loops that once had escalated so much in college that his roommate had asked to be moved. His counselor at MIT worked wonders with this tiny trick of focusing on a word. "Think of the one you choose as zero for your equation. You multiply any situation against it, and things stop. Speak the word and make everything freeze. Like a museum display." Together they had chosen the word "Stay," which seemed logical to Martin, if the goal was a freeze frame, a snapshot, control.

Stay. Stay. Stay. It didn't matter his son was a bitter, mean kid; it didn't matter his greedy wife had cheated on him with someone at the company party; it didn't matter he didn't like his children very much.

Jeremiah refused to leave his room, so Martin took the other two to Mr. Fish. Martin disliked every entrée on the menu—fried this, fried that—as he only ate grilled meat. He ordered a pitiful house salad that came coated with ranch and left it untouched while Bobby ate the Shrimp Poppers and Stephen Alex had the Clam Slam Jam.

"Dad, what about J?" Stephen said as they paid the check.

"We've got bologna at the condo," Martin said.

The sallow-faced, unsmiling teen girl at the register watched them as if she were weighing Martin's abilities as a parent.

"Fine," Martin said. "Order him something."

Stephen Alex smiled as if there were no greater joy than this. His skinny little index finger slid down the greasy plastic menu till he landed on "grilled tilapia plate."

"What?" Martin said. "There's nothing grilled here." But he'd missed it—the one solitary item, severely overpriced— and Stephen Alex nodded with absolute surety that J would want this.

Martin put in the order and they waited almost 15 minutes, an eternity for Bobby, who truly needed something like a leash. Though Martin's gut roiled with hunger, he could not justify the additional $9.99.

Jeremiah ate everything. Martin knew this because when Stephen Alex emerged from the bedroom, nothing remained except a wilted piece of lettuce where the tilapia once sat. Martin picked bologna out of the package and hated his own weakness for giving in to take-out.

"He licked the platter clean!" Stephen Alex announced. It was a rejoicing.

That night Martin dreamed of the hotel where his engineering firm had always held the holiday party, that extravagance of ice sculptures, open bars, and needless dance floors. He remembered two years ago when Kenny and Frank chatted with Marjorie, she a fat little witch in the middle, beaming up at them, baring chubby, available shoulders—how available, he didn't know until too late, what she had done in a dark corner with Kenny. At one point she grabbed him with too much affection, pressing a cheek burning with heat and drink against his. It would be New Year's Day when she would leave with the boys and never return. That shameless flirting—she made him look like a fool—and the worse betrayal—she thought him too foolish to ever find out—yet she was rosy, soft, and scented that night, every night. An endless loop of dream words rolled: *hussy, smack her, head on a platter!*

He woke in a sweat, sat up on his elbows, and glanced at the clock. 3:03 a.m. His heart surged against his chest. Something was wrong. She wasn't next to him.

Of course she wasn't; she hadn't been for over two years. But she was so warm...

Something else was wrong; he didn't know what. But he felt it like blood in his veins. He would go and count heads.

Jeremiah's door was closed but once opened, light from the hall showed that he was sprawled sideways across the bed, long limbs flung out like he had fallen from a great height.

The other room was especially dark since it had no windows. Martin squinted several times, letting in more light from the hall, to see Bobby curled up at the very end of his bed, clutching his teddy. In the other bed, rumpled covers, but no Stephen Alex.

No Stephen Alex.

Martin patted the entire bed, then ducked under. Nothing. He looked under Bobby's bed. He opened the closet. He ran across the hall and did the same in Jeremiah's room. He ran to the bathroom. Then he ran around the entire condo, opening every closet, every cupboard, even those too small for Stephen Alex, till his breath was so ragged he could hardly stand.

The balcony!

Martin dashed to the sliding door. It rumbled ominously

as he opened it. Wet, thick air met him on the tiles as he stumbled out in his bare feet, tripping on the boys' damp towels. He peered over the rail—at least a twenty-foot drop—but saw only an empty lawn and a trickling fountain below, dim forms in the faint, cloud-muddied moonlight. No broken, crumpled body. Streetlights in the parking lot glowed dull and stupid.

He ran to Jeremiah's room and stood over him, still sleeping like the dead.

"Jeremiah." He shook him. "Jeremiah. J!"

Jeremiah woke with a start and sat straight up. "What?" he yelled.

"Calm down. Your brother is missing."

Jeremiah's eyes looked big and white, shining wide as a doll's in the darkness.

"Stay with Bobby. I'm going outside, I'll start looking, and—" Martin realized he could not say where he was going and when he would be back. He tapped his hip, realized he still had boxers on, and said, "I'll get my cell. Call me if he shows up. Just stay here—*do not leave.* I'll be back soon as I can."

"Okay," Jeremiah said. "Do you want me to get Bobby?"

"No, let him sleep." Martin ran from the room.

He found his cell, keys, and wallet, and made for the front door.

"Dad!" called J.

"What?"

"Try the beach."

His heart sank to his stomach as he locked the door. This morning, when they were driving back from the beach, J had sneered, "You didn't even get out there today, and you're going to be a *triathlete*? Whatever."

"I am," Stephen Alex had said firmly, yet without rancor and no detectable pride. When Martin glanced in the

13

rearview mirror, Stephen Alex wore a small, private smile, like someone else, an entity beyond the car, was speaking to him.

As Martin got in the car, streaks of heat lightning stabbed the sky. Thick air clogged his throat; he heard his breath through his open mouth. He looked up and saw J peering over the balcony, his thin body like a paper doll against the condo blazing with light.

He made a slow tour of the parking lot—maybe Stephen Alex still wandered out here—but nothing. Goddammit, the odds—the odds weren't good he'd find him this way. He needed help, but J was too young...He should call the police, but what if Stephen Alex was swimming at the beach, right now—about to drown?

Martin spun out of the complex onto the main road, disobeying every stoplight, till he could turn left toward the shore and park at the first beach access, the place where they had been this morning. Marjorie's cry rang in his ears: "You've let my son drown!"

He threw himself out of the car and tore through the blackness up the splintery stairs toward the roar of high tide. Her vitriol pounding him and his lungs burning, Martin stumbled through cool pillows of sand, screaming, "Stephen Alex!"

The wind here stirred like a restless animal, whipping up whitecaps in the faint moonlight. Martin stumbled right, then left, wishing he had a flashlight, something to identify lifeless shapes slumped here, there, yet revealing nothing as he drew closer. Firm sand beneath his feet now, then a cool film of water, shivers down his spine. No one, nothing—"Stephen Alex!" he cried.

Then he saw something in the black water, about a hundred yards away. He ran at the small form wading waist deep in the swirling dark, a little white head, shoulders, chest floating and bobbing on the waves. Martin charged through the water, his foot snagging on something, his breath ragged, his voice cracking with his child's name.

Stephen Alex, buffeted by the waves, looked his way, and Martin thought he saw him smile.

"Daddy!"

"Stephen Alex, don't move, I'm coming!" Martin heard himself sob.

"Dad, it's okay. Don't be scared!"

Stephen Alex stretched out his hand and Martin caught it. He clutched the boy in his arms, almost falling over as water hit his waist. Then the bottom sank below him, water sucking at their limbs, willing him into the deep. He stumbled again. Stephen Alex felt like a long wet stone in his arms.

He dragged the boy through unstable pockets of grasping sand till they reached ankle-deep water. He let Stephen Alex slip from his arms and sank to his knees, his heart racing so hard he thought he might die.

Stephen Alex looked down at him. "Daddy, are you okay?"

Martin couldn't speak.

"Daddy, why were you so scared?"

Martin could only shake his head.

"I like the water now." Stephen Alex glanced around, eyes searching, as if he'd heard a voice elsewhere. "It's about sixty-five degrees and the wind's only five knots."

Martin nodded, his breath like a roar in his chest. He tried to gulp it back, but it snarled out.

"Don't ever do that again," he croaked. "Please. Don't."

Stephen Alex said, "Daddy, the tide was only four-point-one feet at 3:27 a.m. yesterday, which I think is now."

"Yes," Martin said.

"And a swimmer like me can't die, especially if I'm ready for the triathlon."

Martin believed him. This shadow of himself, his son, was obsessed with height, depth, and breadth just as he was, and pointed like a steel arrow into the future. Do the thing, whatever gripped your mind—that was all that mattered, and everything else be damned. Only this boy had a heart for people in a way Martin would never understand. The moon emerged from behind a cloud and shone down hard on them, bringing all their edges into focus.

"Tomorrow will you swim with me?" Stephen Alex said. "Because I'll need a partner."

Martin gulped down a surge of tears and nodded.

"Let's go, Dad," Stephen Alex said, stretching out his hand.

Martin realized he was sitting, the boy was standing, and like a man, the child was asking him to come home.

MY GRANDMA IS A RACIST

THEY'RE FIGHTING AGAIN, GRANDMA AND Sunny. Cindy and I are secretly taping them from behind the couch. Grandma's visiting from North Carolina, and when she comes over, she brings her bottle of wine. She's mad because Sunny hasn't made dinner yet. Grandma says, and I quote, "Not even any gluten-free crap in this food-free zone." Unquote.

I whisper to Cindy, "Grandma gets mad when she can't get her wine by five. She lets me sip it sometimes but it's nasty."

Cindy whispers back, "My mom would lay down and die and then come back from the dead to wring my neck if I ever drank."

Sunny yells, "What do you know, Mother? Your diet's full of trans fats! You'll pickle your liver with high-fructose corn syrup!"

"I'm sixty-four and healthy as a horse," Grandma says. "Why change now?"

Cindy whispers, "So is your mom going to cook?"

"She likes to wait and see if Grandma will take us out."

"Why doesn't she cook?"

"She says women have to make choices and domesticity is not hers."

Cindy shrugs. I don't think she knows what domesticity is. Dictionary.com never explains anything good, so I guess it means something about making dinner. I can spell it perfectly now.

Now they're fighting about politics. Their voices are louder than the bald guy who screams at the bow tie guy on TV. Sunny yells, "George Bush and Fox News have brainwashed you to fear Muslims!"

Grandma snorts and we hear the wine bottle go pop. When Grandma drinks, the fighting slows down. I whisper to Cindy, "Since George Bush started running against that John Kerry guy the fighting's gotten worse. They fight on the phone and whenever she comes to visit. Sunny's not a huge fan of John Kerry but she says anyone's better than George Bush because he lied to start the war."

"Don't say that to my dad," Cindy says. "I've got cousins in Iraq."

"But it's the truth."

"I wouldn't say it if you want any more dinner at our house." Cindy's mom makes really good tacos and spaghetti and chicken. I eat there as much as I can.

"Sunny hates Grandma's quote-unquote Southern-fried values."

"Why do you keep saying 'quote-unquote'?"

"You know! Because I'm going to do the news, you goof-a-saurus! I've wanted to ever since I was in Sunny's stomach."

"You weren't in her stomach, you were in her woom."

"Woom, baby nest, whatever."

"Baby nest?" Cindy's eyebrows get real high.

Then she has to act all smart and say how the man does stuff with his thing which gives a woman the fish sperm to mate with the egg and then the fetus grows nine months like a bean plant in the big-whup woom. I say, "Who told you this?"

Cindy says, "My mom. She says it's just biology." Cindy

looks all proud, like she knows more science than me. "They'll tell us all about it next year in Health."

"What if the egg cracks?"

"It's not like an *egg*-egg, goof-a-rama! It's like, I don't know, a soft one."

"Is it free range?"

"You don't know anything, do you?" Cindy says. She doesn't say it mean but like she's surprised.

"Shut up! Sunny says I'm gifted!"

"I don't mean that kind of smart." But she can't explain what she means and Cindy never wants to fight so we leave to go act out *Harry Potter and the Prisoner of Azkaban*.

The next fight between Grandma and Sunny is the next day and it gets kind of bad. It's worse because Cindy's not here. Maybe also because they're super mad or maybe because like Grandma says it's hotter than a match inside this house. Grandma paid the morgige but she won't pay the electric. Sunny says it's global warming making things this hot and that where we live here in California used to be desert and to be sure and be super nice to Grandma so we can get a little more money. Grandma's already had a lot of wine, I think before she got here, and she's talking vociferously. I just learned that one. So I go turn on the TV to get away from them. I'd rather watch the worst thing ever, like Marilyn Manson, than hear them scream like this. I wish I could just go to Cindy's, Cindy's, Cindy's.

Grandma keeps yelling, "Lydia, people have been *killed*." She means 9/11. I was only seven then and we all cried because Teacher Larry at my Montessori was crying. Lydia is Sunny's real name. I asked Sunny when do I get to pick mine and she says when I'm eighteen. I don't see why that's a reason to wait when she says I'm smart as hell at ten and almost eleven. I will pick either Asteria or Klymene. These are Greek goddesses no one else even thinks about being on Halloween. Asteria is the goddess of falling stars. Or, I will pick Klymene because she's the goddess of fame, and one day I'll be a famous journalist and writer. I'll have lines around the block at Barnes & Noble like J.K. Rowling. I'll put A.R.D or K.R.D on my books because I think my name would look weird—Wendy Redbird Dancing. But Sunny says it has destinction.

Sunny yells at Grandma, "Mother, we were attacked because we are *hated*! Our CIA has killed people around the world!"

Grandma yells, "Please! Do you think these ragheads give a flying fig? They hate us because we're rich and we're happy and because we let women wear bikinis. These people need to stop throwing rocks and grow something. Ha! They can't, because they live in sand!"

Grandma pours herself another glass. She told me one time that's her victory lap. I guess she means like a winner's drink, like the way our oldest foster cat Slytherin laps up milk real happy after he's beat up the new kitten, Gryffindor.

Sunny says, "Mother, doesn't it bother you we were told there were weapons of mass destruction but now they can't find them? If you follow your logic, we ought to be 'kicking ass' in Afghanistan. That's where bin Laden is, right? Why the hell are we in Iraq?"

"Saddam Hussein is a criminal," Grandma says. "We caught him like a rat in a hole and that's how his days should end: six feet under. But first we need to hang him high."

"Thousands of Iraqis are dying because of us!"

"Three thousand Americans died—and they matter more than a bunch of rich fools who keep women as slaves!"

"Jesus, Mother—that's Saudis. I'm talking about Iraqis!"

Sunny looks at me like I shouldn't be hearing this. Now I'm watching something about the bunny girls but keeping it real low because if Grandma sees all those big boobs she may come over and take the remote. Sunny says women should be proud of their bodies, but she does have a problem with all that sillycone. What I don't understand is why those girls like a really old man. Sometimes I wonder if my real dad is like Hugh in a castle somewhere living with other wives and maybe daughters. What if there's an Asteria Redbird Dancing already, or even a Klymene? What if he named some other girl Wendy?

Grandma walks over to me, trips on my Dance Dance Revolution pad, but catches herself. She pats me on the head. I hate that; why can't she hug? She says she's heard enough, she's starving, and it's time to go.

After she drives off, Sunny comes and wraps her arms around me for a long time. Her eyes are full. Maybe she's thinking about the kids in Darfoor or the polar bears on the icebergs. Then she says, "Wendy, your grandmother is a racist."

I say, "I know, Mom." I like to call her Mom when she's thinking about something else; plus, I get to sound like other kids when I do that.

Sunny says, "Do you have any Muslims in your class?"

"No, I don't think so." Fifth grade's been pretty cool because I got to be friends with all the kids except Dustin Sanchez who used to chase me and now sucker punches me if I walk too close too him, but that's because he's obsessed with me. I like a whole list of boys, each for different things, even though most of them act crazy stupid.

I guess Sunny's still thinking about the Muslims when she says, "Do kids make fun of kids who wear different clothes?"

"Yeah, one time some dude said something to Adeeb because he wears a turban. But he's a Seek which is not a Muslim so he has to. He used to carry that dagger but they took it away and he—"

"Sweetie, it's not a dagger, it's a ceremonial sword, a *kerpan*. Don't *ever* say 'dagger'; that's very offensive to a Seek."

"Like 'raghead'?"

"Oh, God, yes, especially 'raghead.' So you heard that? Goddammit." Sunny starts muttering to herself.

"It's okay, Mom," I say. "Don't worry." Sunny is always upset about bad stuff happening somewhere else, so if she and Grandma fight on top of that it's like she might lose her mind.

Sunny goes to call one of her friends. There might not be dinner tonight, so I go to my laptop and look up *kerpan*. It takes me four tries to spell it right—kir, not ker, kerr, kur, kurr—but I finally find it—*kirpan*—on the KidHunt Encyclopedia. It's also Sikh not Seek.

The kirpan is a weapon that Sikhs may use for defense and it is also a symbol. First, it can be a tool of "ahimsa" or non-violence. Ahimsa is a belief that people should actively prevent violence rather than stand by watching it happen. The kirpan may be used to stop violence from hurting a defenseless person when all other methods have been tried. As a symbol, the kirpan represents the power of truth to cut through lies.

———— ∘∘⟨⟩∘∘ ————

It makes sense Sunny likes Sikhs because she's all about ahimsa. She told me about the lunch counters and the fire hoses and the dogs, which happened like over ten years before I was born. But I guess she wouldn't agree with a Sikh stabbing a dog even if it was biting to be racist.

I told Cindy one time about how people used to be super racist. She said her grandma who lives in Alabama already told her all about it because she couldn't drink out of the water fountains.

I said, "How did she not die of thirst?"

"Well, there was a white one and a black one, and she got the black one."

"Like black water? Ewww."

"No, goofus, it was different fountains for the different races."

I tried to picture all this. "I like your skin better than mine," I said. "Yours is smooth and looks like a candy bar."

Cindy said I looked like an egg with a little bit of a tan. Sunny says my dad was a Native American, a Zuni, which is why I tan so good, and she left him behind on the reservation because he was not into child reering, so that's why she did it alone, plus she knows she does a better job than a man. On the video of my birth she's holding me tight and saying, "I made you all by myself."

I go to the kitchen and turn on the fan real high because Sunny can't run the air conditioning unless Grandma gives us more money. Sunny says the secret to getting what you want is thinking like you already have it. Like we need to imagine a house that's cool and a new Prius and Sunny getting her em-f-ay in mixed-up media and a trip to Busch Gardens so I can ride on Apollo's Chariot with its 210-foot drop. Sunny says world peace would be good, too.

I eat some rice crackers and drink some orange juice, and that's pretty much all I need because the heat kind of takes my appetite away.

The next day, which is the last day of school, Grandma picks me up because Sunny's doing grass roots. Right at the drop-off circle is Adeeb and his family. His dad looks just like him but with a bigger turban and his mom has her hair in a bun on the back of her head with a scarf over it. She's very pretty; her skin is like a soy lattay. I wait for Grandma to say something, but she doesn't. Finally I say, "Hey, look, Grandma, ragheads."

Grandma has rented a new Lexus and she's punching her CD player, so it takes her a second to look up.

"Don't say that."

"But you say ragheads."

"Stop your sassing. That's a terrible habit, thanks to your mother. You're not an adult and won't be for ages."

I think, *That's not true!* but don't say it. I can tell she's watching Adeeb hug his baby sister and climb into their big silver minivan. They look like the other families here except for the stuff on their heads.

Grandma puts her Frank Sinatra CD in the player and lets him sing most of "All of Me" while we crawl through the traffic to get out of the circle. It will take us like fifteen minutes which Sunny says is one of the crimes of suburbeea but it never bothers Grandma which is why Sunny tries to make her do it all the time.

Grandma says, "It's just an expression. I'm talking about bad people who kill Americans. *Those* are ragheads."

"Like Osama bin Laden?"

"Like Osama bin Laden."

"Do you think we'll catch him?"

"We always do. We're a sleeping giant. If you wake us, you pay the piper." Grandma's mouth gets very tight, like she might go fight him.

"What's the piper?"

"You don't know the Pied Piper?"

I do my puppy-dog face, so she says, "It's just a fairy tale. This town hires the piper to kill all the rats. He plays his pipe, they follow him into the river, and they all drown. The town doesn't pay him, so he plays the pipe again. This time, all the children follow him into the river. They all drown. There you have it. Pay your bills on time, or else."

"Why did he do it? That's totally cruel and unusual."

"It's what they call revenge, also known as the IRS."

"So if you don't pay the piper, then you pay...with your life!"

"Exactly. Smart girl." Grandma inches the car up.

I was going to say, "But that's a human rights violation," but I don't because I'm kind of like amazed: Grandma never compliments me. I heard her tell Sunny one time she thought I was smart, but then Grandma said, "But that's no excuse to treat her like she's thirty. She needs some rules." So I guess to her I'm not really that smart. She has no idea how much I know.

I say, "Did you know Michael Jackson has a painting in his mansion where he's playing a pipe with kids following him? I saw it on the E Channel."

"He has a what?" Grandma shakes her head. "That man is loony tunes."

"He's had his nose done like twenty ways."

"The man used to be black." Grandma sighs. "We live in terrible times, let me tell you."

I say, "I want to be embed with the troops."

"What? What are you saying?" She looks horrified.

"I want to be embed with the troops. You know, report on the front lines? For the war?" I almost say, *"Duh!"* like I do to Sunny, but one time I did that, and Grandma pinched me so hard I cried.

"Oh." I've never seen Grandma look relieved and now she does, like really relieved. I don't know why. Being embed is still very dangerous.

I say, "Don't you know, I'm going to be like Anderson Cooper?"

"That's not safe for a girl," she says.

I roll my eyes at the window. Wait till Sunny hears *that.*

"What's this new boyfriend I keep hearing about?" Grandma says.

"I don't like any boys." Lying to Grandma is dangerous, but she does not need to know about the five boys I like or even about crazy Dustin Sanchez.

"No, no, I mean your mother."

"She doesn't have one yet." Usually she does, but they don't stay more than a few weeks.

"Well, she told me she was meeting Nelson something or other."

"No, she's doing Global Hearts."

Grandma snorts. She doesn't like Sunny's grass roots. "There's some new man, I'm certain of it. Lord help us, this revolving door."

I don't know what a revolving door is, but looking at Grandma's face I don't want to ask.

Now we're *finally* pulling out of the circle onto the main road. I yell, waving, "Bye, bye, Cambridge, you baby-schmaby school! See ya! *Lay*-tah! Don't need you no' mo'!" I talk black, TV black, not Cindy black, to see if I can get Grandma mad.

"So you think you're grown now?"

"I'm a *sixth* grader! I'm in *middle school*."

"You wait. You'll be bottom of the heap next year."

I hate it when she tries to diss me. Grandma tells Sunny kids should be seen but not heard and I say totally the opposite. Sunny says kids have the most wisdom of all. Sunny always told me every Christmas my gifts came from her while Grandma said it was Santa Claus. They got in a big fight about it when I was five. Sunny says she treats children with respect and doesn't indulge in myths.

We come back to our house and Sunny isn't there yet. Grandma grumbles about the yard, all the weeds and how ugly the tragedy mask is, the one from Sunny's favorite artist that's nailed to our big, dead hickory tree. Grandma says it all should be kindling. When we get inside, Grandma counts the balls of cat hair floating around—orange, white, and black. I watch her look for a dishrag to clean the counters so she can make me a snack, and the whole time she acts like there's boogers everywhere. In North Carolina Grandma lives in a fancy place behind walls with a sleepy security guard, so our place isn't up to her snuff. She makes me a soy butter sandwich and gives me a glass of soy milk and says there's no real food here. We sit and watch Nickelodeon. I don't tell Grandma I never watch that, ever.

Then the front door bangs, and it's Sunny with some other voice. This new man walks into our TV room.

As soon as I see him, I think of a shaggy dog. Maybe it's because he has long hair over his ears and black eyes and a gray chin. His shoulders are big but his legs are short. He leans kind of left. He's looking at me like I am a fillay mean yon. Sunny says that when she's really hungry, like she could eat the world or a fillay mean yon. It must mean a really big piece of tofu, since that's her favorite protein.

Sunny says, "Sweetie, come here. This is Nelson. Give him a hug."

For some reason Grandma puts out her hand, like we stopped fast in the Lexus and she doesn't want me going through the windshield. But then she lets me go.

When he hugs me, he grunts and presses my face into his belly button. I smell cigarettes in his shirt and something really sour. I can't wait to get away.

I go sit on the sofa and turn the TV up really, really loud.

"Wendy!" Grandma says. She grabs the remote and scratches me with her long nails.

"I don't care!" I yell. "Sunny never got me the recorder! I like asked till I lost my mind!" I was going to transcry everything people said word for word and start being a journalist.

"Good Lord, you've raised a brat." Grandma snaps off the TV. "What's she want now?"

"Baby girl, I'll get it for you, I promise. My little Anderson Cooper!" But Sunny is looking at Nelson who's looking at me.

"You're full of bull," I say. I turn the TV back on.

Sunny looks at Nelson and shakes her head. Then she says with her lips but no voice, "Kids."

"I see you!" I yell.

She claps her hands like she doesn't hear me. "Party, party, party!" She says to Nelson, "Love, I want to introduce you to *everybody*."

Grandma snorts. She says low so only I hear, "What are we up to, number five this year?" I hate her, but then I wish she would come sit with me on the sofa right now; I don't know why. The way Nelson is looking at me is kind of like how Dustin Sanchez's eyes follow me all around the school, only I don't know that I can stick my tongue out or tell Nelson he's a dumbass.

Sunny grabs the phone and starts leaving messages for Britta, Fender, Tree Harmony, Niobe, and Bellicosa.

Grandma says kind of angry, "Well, I'll be on my way." She gives me a look like, "Good luck with these yahoos."

Sunny doesn't notice that Grandma's leaving because she's in my bedroom talking to somebody on her phone.

I flip to VH1. It's *Behind the Music*, about these '80s dudes with makeup and big hair. I like old stuff.

Nelson sits down next to me. At first his smell stuffs up my nose but then I start getting used to it. He starts laughing down deep in his throat when he sees what I'm watching.

"So, Wendy Redbird Dancing, are you a music fan?" He talks to me like Sunny does, like I'm his age.

"I listen to everything." I turn the sound up a little.

He laughs real low again, looking at the TV. He points at

the screen as the band name comes up: Mötley Crüe. "You know those dots? They're called u-m-l-a-u-t-s: umlauts." Then he tells me how he plays guitar.

I don't say anything, because there's a story about someone choking on barf and then dying and I don't know how someone could do that.

"I could teach you," he says. "I'm playing for the Kerry campaign."

"Maybe. Sunny's sending me to Girls Rock this summer." It's a rock band camp and then I'm going to drama camp with Cindy and then I get to go with her and her family to the beach maybe for like a whole week. It's going to be an *awesome* summer.

"Sweet," he says. He looks impressed, and I feel kind of proud. "Maybe I can come see you rock out."

I shrug because I don't know what else to say. He probably won't be around when Girls Rock starts.

"Gum?" he says, and pulls out this kind I've never seen.

I take a stick. It's got little speckles on it—green and pink. I bite down and it like explodes. My cheeks suck in like my mouth just collapsed. It's what I think Apollo's Chariot will be, but only in your mouth.

"Pretty good, huh?" He grins and chomps too. When he smiles he has a nice face.

Sunny comes back in, talking real fast on the phone, but she notices us sitting next to each other and she gets this big smile, bigger than I've seen in a long time. It's like her face melts and she's all happy, and then I'm happy, and all of a sudden I think, *Maybe this guy is the one who'll stay.* He just needs to take more baths and shave his chin and Sunny won't like the smoking, but she says she likes to help people change themselves.

While Sunny's friends start coming in I go hide in my room with the phone. I call Cindy, but she's crying.

"What's wrong?"

"We have to go to Paris." Her dad is a professor and goes to all these other countries and then he writes books there. One time they went to Coat DeeVar, which is in Africa, but they stayed like only a month. I wish I lived with them.

"The whole summer?"

Cindy sniffs. She never cries, so this is bad.

"Maybe I can come visit," I say. "I know French." Sunny let me see the movie about Paris and I learned the voolez voo song. I just have to figure out a way to get Sunny to get Grandma to pay for the trip.

"I can't do camp with you," she says.

My stomach sinks to the bottom of my feet and I start to cry, too. "Can't we go to the beach?"

"No," she says, and she's sobbing.

I say, "I'll come visit, I promise!" I hate her crying; I want to make it stop like I want to make Sunny's stop.

There's a tap on the door.

Cindy says, "I don't know. I have to go."

"I want to sleep over tomorrow, make your parents let me, okay?"

"Okay. Bye." I get off and go open the door. It's Nelson.

He sees my face and he gets this look like he's starving when he sees me sad. He wipes the tears off my cheek with a finger, and it feels strange, but good. I don't know any dudes who have soft fingers. He looks like he should have rough hands, motorcycle or car mechanic hands, but he doesn't.

Behind him are all Sunny's friends in our TV room sitting on the floor. They're talking in loud voices about John Kerry and grass roots. They're passing a bottle of wine and eating hummus with broccoli.

He shuts the door and it's quieter. "Why are you crying?" he says.

"My best friend is leaving me all summer."

"Aw." He sits on my bed and pats it. "Sit down. Let's talk."

I sit next to him, not too close, even though I like getting close to people. Sunny's dudes always pretend to talk to me but only because they want to know about her or where she keeps the pot, and when I say, "in the kitchen by the stove," they get bored and go away.

"Who is your friend?" he says.

"Cindy."

"How old is she?"

"She's three months younger but she's real smart and she never tells secrets. I almost told hers one time to Ruth, but then I remembered just in time that Cindy never tells. The other girls are all fake and go tell your stuff but Cindy and I are BFFs and we're like really close. Sunny wants to know everything Cindy says, but I am so not telling her how Cindy likes Jeremy." Then I realize I'm kind of like starting to tell things, so I stop.

I look up and Nelson's got this funny expression like he's even happier. I don't know what I'm saying that makes him so happy, but it's fun to have someone to talk to. Sunny just doesn't have the time anymore, because of this difficult campaign.

"Who are your friends?" I say.

"Guys don't have friends. I like to stay on the move." He pulls out a set of keys and dangles them in front of me. "See, I got this motorcycle, baby, and she takes me wherever I need to go."

"That's hot," I say, just like Paris Hilton.

Nelson cracks up. Then he starts rubbing my back, just beneath my neck. It feels really good. Like maybe this is what those massages are Sunny always goes to get.

I jump off the bed. "Want to see my NetPets?" I pull out my two big boxes from my closet. "I have like fifty." I start telling him about how they have a high-security code and you can enter it at the web site, and then you can play with your virtual pet for hours. I've won all the points though, so they need to improve their games. I turn on my laptop to start to show him, but he says, "Nah, maybe later."

"But they're velllllllve-ty soooooft," I say, just like the commercial, rubbing Uni-Tunes, the unicorn, on my cheek. He holds out his hands and I toss it to him. I have seven of the ten mythical beasts and all I have left to get is the griffin, the jabberwocky, and the gremlin. The worst is the pixie. They put pink hair and a bikini and high heels on her, and I agree with Grandma—she's ugly as sin. Maybe Hugh Hefner would like her though.

Nelson is rubbing Uni-Tunes on his cheek just like I do, and he looks like he might fall asleep. Maybe he has narkaleprosy like Cindy's grandpa.

"Do you believe in mythical beasts?" I ask.

"What?"

"Like unicorns? Sometimes I think there might have been griffins once upon a time and they just killed them off."

"I don't know. There's some pretty crazy stuff out there," he says. "One time I saw a cow with two heads."

"No!"

"Yep. I was working this farm and the mama cow had a calf. Two heads, but the tongues worked at the same time because they shared a brain."

"Wow." Then I realize he might have been places I want to go. "Hey, have you been to Africa or Paris?"

He grins. "Nah, but I've seen a lot of secret places."

"Tell me!"

"Well, then they wouldn't be secret."

"Can you take me?" Maybe where he goes is near Paris where Cindy will be.

"If you're good," he says. That's weird because he

doesn't seem like he's a discipleranarian and Sunny doesn't like discipleranarians either. "So you must like secrets."

"I love secrets! But Sunny *never* lets me have any!"

"Can you keep mine?"

"Of course!"

"I don't know, you're kind of young." He says it, but I can tell he doesn't believe it.

"I am almost *eleven*. I'm in *middle school*."

"All right, then. Maybe when we know each other better."

"Do you like *Super Smart Kids*? That's the best show and I get all the questions right."

"Sure, sure."

I make him promise he'll watch it with me when it comes on.

I tell Sunny after he leaves that he and I may share secrets if he's really lucky and she says, "That's cool." Then I say, "But I hope it's not something lame like Santa Claus and the Easter Bunny." She rolls her eyes and says, "I know, right?" but she's not really listening. She has some people she has to call because Nelson is helping her with a concert and plus, her friends always leave a big mess, so she's running around cleaning.

It's way hot. Cindy doesn't call. Our air conditioning's messed up. I can't sleep good. I pull off everything except my underwear but the air is so stuffy I can't hardly breathe. I have very weird dreams, most of them about Grandpop, and he's looking very mad. Grandpop got kind of scary before he died. He made me read the Bible with him every day whenever we visited North Carolina. I didn't like that at all. He made me memorize verses and Grandma said I had to keep him busy because he was driving her nuts, so I sat with him and repeated weird stuff like "'...out of men's hearts, come evil thoughts, blahblahblah blah, all these evils come from inside...' Mark 7:21-23." I looked up all the words I didn't know, like lewdness, and I pretty much did not need to know about that. Sunny got so mad when she heard. She cussed out Grandpop, then Grandma, and then the onions she was chopping. She cried into them for a good long time.

———————

Today is a good day because it is July 24, 2004, which means I am finally eleven. It's been a pretty good summer because basically I have a new pal even though Cindy left. Cindy's written me like five postcards and one even in French because she's smart as me, but even smarter with languages. I've sent her one letter, and a bunch of e-mails to her dad's Yahoo. Her parents still won't let her do MySpace. I tell Nelson all about everything she says except her secret thoughts about cute French boys. One even kissed her on the lips but it only lasted like a second. I think Nelson might be okay to tell sometime because it's kind of like telling a dad, if I had one. He's stayed like four and a half weeks now, which is a record. My Zuni dad can go freak himself, I don't believe in him at all anyway. I looked up Zuni on all these web sites and those people have square old faces and look like someone walked all over them, and they're wearing turbans. I don't look a thing like any of those raghead people.

Nelson says we're buds. He likes the same cartoons I do; he sneaks me Reese's Puffs instead of Sunny's quinoa cereal, and he always watches *Super Smart Kids* and *SpongeBob* with me. He likes my stories I write about griffins and stunt girls. The best one that I read him is "Where in the world is Wendy?" which is about this journalist who goes with Anderson Cooper everywhere and helps people get the word out about natural disasters and war tore up countries.

He doesn't get crazy about politics, even though he helps with the cam pain. I think that's great.

So this day that I am eleven, of course Sunny and Grandma, who came back for a two-day visit just to see me but whatever, she's so mean, well, they have their biggest fight ever. They are mad about flip-flops and Swiffer boats and the campaign and they are basically shrieking. Nelson comes out of the bathroom and I'm sure he couldn't go, there was such a racket, and he says, "Ladies, ladies. Can we call a truce today?"

Grandma says her time is better spent on the right coast and huffs and puffs and blows her way out.

"See?" Sunny says to Nelson, and tears hang off her lashes, "You see what I deal with. The *bigotree.*"

Nelson is looking at me, so Sunny looks and says, "And Wendy's birthday—how does that make her feel? The selfishness!"

Nelson winks at me like it's all okay. I hide a grin behind my hand. Our secret is that Grandma and Sunny are red and blue and crazy all over.

He hugs Sunny and says, "Babe, you deserve a break. Go do something for yourself. Wendy and I need to celebrate her birthday together and then the big dinner tonight." He gives me a thumbs up and I'm happy again.

"Eleven!" Sunny sings. "My little dancing redbird! What a young woman you are."

I smile with mystery. I am only seven years away from being Asteria or Klymene but I bet I can convince Sunny to let me change it, now that I'm eleven.

Mother goes to tea with her best girlfriends (she has six now), and she says she's going to check out the craft class at the arts center.

Nelson and I drive to the park. It's only ten o'clock

but it's so hot you can fry an egg on the sidewalk, he says. He lets me take off the seat belt so I can sit right next to him like Sunny, because he agrees with her child reering philosofee. You don't ever let the child go till they want to leave you. Sunny says she never let go of me till I was three. She says we're all the same energy anyway. Grandma says I'm clingy all the time, so I never try it with her anymore. Sunny told me to tell anybody who says anything, "That's right, I'm like lint on black pants," and walk away with my head held high.

He plays me these rap songs he says I should know, like this one about let your booty go smack. It's like totally hot. We get to the park and he puts the car pretty far from the playground, like we'll have to walk a ways. I sit up tall and see this little girl over on the slide and her dad is chasing her near the swings and she's screaming. I want to yell at her, *Ha ha, I have a dad now too!*

I grab for the door handle. He puts out his hand.

"Not yet," he says. "Let's just sit here. Check things out."

I look out the window. I watch the little girl. She shrieks so loud she could break glass. I think I'm too big for the slide. Kinda sorta, but I'll try it.

He says, "Ticklefest?"

I shrug whatever. I'd rather go outside. He tickles around my waist like he always does in front of Sunny. Now his hand goes farther down, down, down. At first it feels good but then it doesn't because he won't stop, and then he takes my hand. To do things. For I think a long time. I don't really remember. Sometimes people's eyes get dead and flat and you can't see inside.

We come home, and Grandma is sitting on the edge of the sofa, looking mad. "And where have you been?" she says to me, but she's talking to Nelson.

I see her face, and I feel like I'm going to be very sick.

"The park," he says. He looks at Grandma like she's bad.

"She was supposed to be at Y camp. I went there to pick her up, and no Wendy." Grandma smacks the sofa hard; I see swirls of snowy dust and cat hair. She looks at me hard, like I have a secret. "Come here."

I go sit beside her and she yanks me close. This is weird because Grandma is the patting kind who never holds you long. I taste pennies in my throat.

"We're going to the Y," she says, like the morning camp isn't over and I'm too old for that stuff. "Get your suit."

I get my swimsuit because I can't really talk, and we leave without Nelson. He's looking at me when Grandma turns around and his chin is so gray it's black. He's shaking his head at me and I remember the last thing he said in the car, about Sunny and how she'll leave me if I tell.

On the way over, Grandma looks like she wants to ask me something but she doesn't. She just rolls down the window and lights one, then another cigarette. The smoke hurts my throat and I watch the dashboard very hard so I don't throw up in Grandma's car.

At the Y I see Adeeb and his family. He's playing with his sister in the kiddie pool and on his head is a patka. He told me one day in PE what it was. He said it's to keep all the hair he never cuts very tidy. His is blue and it's knotted at the top like a little bun. A boy with a bun. Funny, but not ha-ha funny.

I stay in the deep end because I can tread water for ages and ages. But this time I can't go very long. I ache down there because it was rubbed too hard. I cling to the side of the pool. I see Adeeb smile with very white teeth when he waves at me and the patka is shiny and wet and I think about how I would like a patka, only I'd want it to cover everything in this cool, deep, hiding water.

When I get out Grandma rubs me with a towel real hard like I need to be scrubbed with her Brillo pads and Clorox. She sounds like she's been smoking even though she doesn't smell that way, and she says to me, "What's wrong with you?"

"Nothing."

She says, "Your sorry mother needs to do her job. He's not your babysitter."

I nod.

"We're going to Mass before I leave."

I don't want to fight, so I say for the first time in a long time, "Yes, ma'am."

She looks at me and for some reason she's even more upset. I don't think it's because I'm in trouble. But I should be. I should.

Grandma drops me off in the driveway. I want to ask if she'll come inside and then I want to ask if she thinks Sunny would ever leave me like he said, but now she smokes one, two, three cigarettes, and looks so mad I finally go in by myself.

Mom is back from tea and Nelson is gone. I go to my room to change and I'm smelly and slimy and cold, even though it's like a hundred degrees everywhere. Mom comes into my room and wants to know what we did.

I feel like I'm going to throw up, so I don't talk.

She looks at me weird and says, "What's up, Wendy Redbird?"

"Mom..."

"Yes, what?"

I swallow hard. "I don't know..."

"What?"

"My tummy..."

"Are you sick?"

"...my tummy feels funny when he's around."

She sits next to me on the bed and takes my hand. Her eyes are wet. "Oh sweetie. I know it's hard. It's tough wondering about my boyfriends, isn't it? I'll settle down someday, I promise. You'll have a dad one of these days. If you can just be patient."

"I don't need a dad right now."

"I know you don't, sweetie."

"Mommy?"

"Yes, sweetie, what?"

"Mommy, I'm really bad—"

"No, honey, no, you're not—"

"—but at least I'm not a racist."

"Oh my God, did Grandma say something about sin again? Sweetie, listen to me. Whenever she says that crap, you just tell yourself, 'That's crazy; there's no sin; I'm perfect.'" She grabs me and hugs me hard. "Okay?"

"Okay." But I feel cold inside like I can never get warm.

She winks at me and says we're BFFs.

I feel very sick so I let her go away. I count hard and fast as I can so I won't throw up and when I get to 177 I start feeling better and I start thinking about how someone can sneak on a plane. I wonder how far away Paris is and if Cindy's parents would send me back or if she could somehow hide me. Or even better if I can get Grandma to get Sunny a ticket, too, then we can go to the Eiffel Tower, just the two of us, and no one will get in the middle.

I go find the *Webster's* dictionary Grandma gave me, because she says I'm lazy going on the computer all the time. It's like ancient, like from 1978, when my mom was a kid, and the binding is all cracked. Cindy and I made it our book of spells when we used to play Harry Potter. First I look up "ultimate" then "betrayal." I put the words together like math. I already know betrayal, but I guess he means Sunny will think I am like the most worst unfaithful person ever because of what I did. When people are betrayed they never go back to that person. That person is left alone.

That night when I lie in bed I am frozen. I feel polar-bear air all around my shoulders and behind my ears. I can't sleep because I am very nervous he will be here. Then I remember he works the night shift at the Safeway because it's Thursday, so it's okay.

I still listen just in case he changes his mind.

I will never go to the park again. I'm too old. Now I remember words about wanting things and how he knew I did. I remember his cold voice that made the car go stiff as icicles. How dirty I am. How Mom will hate me forever if she ever finds out.

But we keep going to the park, and there are things even more bad than I thought, when he puts the car really far away from the swings and slide. All the time we go, whenever he stays with us, like whenever Sunny leaves, which is every day. Mom always says it's fine for me to go, though I walk away and kick stuff and make her yell at me. Sometimes I try to hide. I go to the Tenleys' back yard behind their recycling. He always seems to know where I am and find me.

It is August I think maybe...July went so slow I almost died. I can't remember which day it is, especially now when he makes me do stuff in my room.

When school starts I will be away from the house longer each day, which is good. But what if school is really bad like Grandma said it would be. What if quote-unquote bottom of the heap means they push you down and do stuff to you. I heard eighth-graders are really big dudes. But what's worse is at night when I never sleep. I hear noises and I'm waiting for what's next.

In bed at night I think about all the things I am and am not. I am the kid with the highest score on all the end-of-grade tests, or I was. I was the best actress in the whole school and a kickball player and a girl who liked five boys and the fastest speller in the class. I was ten going on eleven but now I am, I don't know, like a million years old.

Grandma comes back to visit just before school starts and takes me one morning to the Y. I see Adeeb. He's going to Warsaw, the same middle school as me.

He waves at me from the shallow end where he's holding up his baby sister with pink floaties on her arms so she can pretend to swim.

I swim over. I look to see where he's got his hands on her—just her tummy—so I feel better. He gives her away to his mom who is reaching for her from the side of the pool.

"Hey," I say. "Want to race to the deep end?"

"Sure," he says. His teeth are super white.

I blast off, but he jets past me. We come up sputtering after what feels like a mile later. I wipe my nose before he can see the snot.

I say, "Do you have your *kirpan*?"

"Nah, I don't take it with me now."

"Can I borrow it?"

He looks surprised. "Why?"

"I don't know, for like, homeland security."

He looks totally confused. "You aren't supposed to use it. It's my religion."

I don't know what to say back, so I duck my head under water. Oh no, oh no—I see his long swim trunks bunching up and I know his thingy's underneath. I'm bad, and I wish I were dead. I snort water up my nose and cough super hard. Then I swim away to the shallow end where only the babies are.

Tonight in bed I'm safe, and to make myself fall asleep I hold my breath as long as I can, so if there is a God, She will know that I don't want a baby, ever, and I am way too young to have one. I haven't seen any fish or eggs. The thingy goes in my mouth so I don't know if you can have a baby that way but maybe you could.

If I had Adeeb's kirpan, I would cut myself a hole in the wood frame around my closet. I would burrow into that black knot I see. That's where I go the nights he comes in here. It will be a tunnel, like under Hogwarts and on top stands a Whomping Willow ready to hit anyone who tries to come after me. If I'm followed through all the twists and turns, I can yell EXPECTO PATRONUM like Harry Potter and then maybe Apollo will appear in his chariot like a fireball.

I am almost asleep, really want sleep, but now it's a kind of sleep I will wake from right away like a cat. I start to see kirpans cutting like a sword. They slice and they dice through a big gray fog spreading everywhere in this house. I hear Grandma shout in the distance, getting farther and farther away, something about the UN and its loosey-goosey negosheeations, everywhere you turn.

3.0

THIS IS ELISABETH IRENE SCHLEGEL on real life. Version 1.0, circa 1978.

If her children come home, she says, "You never visit," words looping like a worn cassette warbling on its reel. Her children roll their eyes and turn the TV up, preferring *M*A*S*H* or *The Price is Right*.

All of them finished college. Elisabeth never finished grade school because reading is so hard. If she picks up a book now, it sends her straight back to times when American kids call her Kraut and mock her knee socks, when teachers sigh as she speaks. To the time after eighth grade when she works her father's sugar beet fields in the heat despite the blinding migraines. It's 1927 when Mr. Castiglione's car breaks down on the highway and he stumbles on her, rosy with sunburn. She is seventeen. A month later, she is pregnant.

For a while her stomach is easy to hide because food has always been a comfort. She's a big girl, the neighbors say, lucky to get a man. Finally, Mr. Castiglione says they should go see the judge. Her parents thank God for one less to feed.

Six children later, Elisabeth wonders if she could ever learn to read, but the headaches, the laundry, the meals. She rifles through paperbacks at the dime store, taking some home on days without headaches. Her eyes rove anywhere but the page, thoughts dancing like a pinball, lighting up corners of her brain. There is no peace.

When Mr. Castiglione dies from a heart attack, he leaves her a big house and the business. She gives the boys the latter. Alone in the house, she thinks about hiring a girl to clean, but that is selfish. The tips of her fingers crack and bleed from Clorox; she shows the children when they visit. She laughs when she makes her spinster daughter cry, the one who left for California and returns once a year. Elisabeth cries when the same daughter tells her years later she's finally found a man. The boys don't call, but at least they didn't leave town with the grandchildren. None of them understands the fields, the pregnancies, the pinball mind, the dreams.

This is Elisabeth Irene Schlegel on education, Version 2.0, where she graduates college. Don't ask how she graduated high school. Just assume that once Mr. Castiglione dies on a sad but blessed day in 1956, his money calls from the bank. She takes some before the boys hear.

Six feet under, Mr. Castiglione gives further permission to hire a cleaning woman. Now Elisabeth reads all day. The woman says, "Mrs. C., I never did understand books," but she doesn't mind Elisabeth reading to her, even with that crazy pacing to keep the mind quiet.

It is a time when beatniks at the university love an older German-Russian peasant émigré. Her professors feed her Hesse and Tolstoy, Plath and Hansberry. Her hunger for words is insatiable.

With early menopause, the migraines pass and she can read for ten minutes straight without losing her mind. It takes her all night to read forty pages, but if she drinks two pots of coffee, she can graduate.

She tries to starve herself but morsels still leave weight

behind. The beatniks shrug: it's not the body but the spirit within. She quits her attendance at St. Mary's; Mass always leaves her winded, the incense smothering until her voice cracks at *Ite, missa est.*

When Elisabeth graduates, her children miss the ceremony. Unseemly, a middle-aged mother graduating college, never mind the selfishness of borrowing against her grandchildren. The spinster daughter still resents things said in 1958 about girls not being worth the college expense, so she schedules her nick-of-time wedding the same day as Elisabeth's graduation, never dreaming there will be plenty of cash when the granddaughter heads to Harvard in 1986. None of the children or grandchildren understands the fields, the pregnancies, the pinball mind, the realized dream.

<hr />

This is Elisabeth Irene Schlegel on dope: Adderall, Imitrex, Synthroid, and Ortho Novum. With Adderall she can read for hours. With Imitrex her head expands, spacious like an old bell; thoughts resonate without pain, without threats of cracking her head, no matter what she eats or smells. With Synthroid she remains a curvy 144 most of her life. With Ortho Novum she never has to suffer labor or ungrateful children.

She graduates college because Mr. Castiglione pities a barren woman who ought to keep busy. When he dies, she leaves for the city and buys an upscale apartment with maid service. The girls they send always leave because Liza insists on paying their college tuition.

She opens a bookstore funded by the sale of Mr. Castiglione's business. The beatniks buy books from her used bin and call her Mama Brecht.

But this is crazy pacing in my pinball mind.

I, her granddaughter, can't feed drugs of a brave new world to the matriarch who suffered to birth my mother. I can't undo my upper middle-class home, Ivy League degree, or lucrative career. Would I forego all this so she could have my life?

A soy pumpkin spice venti latté fuels this revelation here at the Starbucks corner table, one I snatched after a mom with twin toddlers left it a greasy shambles. The city day outside is gray and slimy with rain, heads bent in relentless strides toward productivity. I pocket my CrackBerry and pop an Excedrin Migraine so I can think in a straight line, seeking a stillness I can't quite name. I pull out my journal and fumble in an oversized, overloaded bag for a pen.

My sufferings won't pay Gramma's debts—not even the soulless one-night stands, my childless and defunct marriage, and all the working weekends. I see shrinks and dither high at the apex of Maslow's pyramid. I understand what I escaped: the fields, the pregnancies, the pinball mind.

Version 1.0 is how it happened. Suffering. Version 2.0 is only possible if Gramma dared to follow a strange dream with sheer and staggering will.

Is 3.0 what I call progress? Yes, remember the maids... Elisabeth could have helped twenty through college. Instead she helped me.

I don't like this math.

Yet if Elisabeth became something so fit, I'd be extinct.

Am I worth the sacrifice? Not a husband's heifer, not a children's lamb for the slaughter, I'm too fit for my own good.

Unless God wants to arrange another incarnation—and

wrestle me to bring it to term—I see only one option for this medicated, manicured body of mine.

I pick up my pen and begin to write.

In memory of Katherine Irene Schlegel Fuoco. 1904-1983

RETROGRADE

"IT WAS NOTHING, WHAT WE saw last night," Freda told Neal as they left the town limits of Chapel Hill. "Nothing but a Russian booster rocket."

"That spectacular blaze?" Neal said.

"Here I thought it was so auspicious." She hated it wasn't a meteor burning iron to death, a symbol of creative transformation, like a phoenix. The list of dreams she jotted last night, hopes for her future, seemed silly in the face of this fact—that the fire in the sky was only space junk.

"Auspicious how?" He didn't look critical, though he always rolled his eyes at her astrology. She would say he looked inquisitive.

She said, "Certain Native Americans venerated the rocks, and the Ka'ba at Mecca is meteorite. It's where heaven meets earth."

"I don't know about that there rock worshippin'. Us Chreestchins don't cotton to that."

He winked at her and she laughed. A good sign; he was loosening up. He pointed the car west toward Wilmington and took her hand. She squeezed back, remembering the thrill of last night, loving how her fingers locked with his. At times like these, his strange religious conversion seemed forever away—a story of thirty-five years spent dodging his family's fire-and-brimstone dogma while living the life of a debauched, alcoholic writer, until one day he heard a song at a bluegrass festival that somehow delivered Jesus to his door. When he'd met her, he was two years sober and two years Christian. In the six months they'd been together, he'd tried only one time to quote Scripture at her, in their first two weeks of dating. She'd nipped that in the bud right away, saying, "I prefer Rumi, Buddha, and the astrologer DivinaTerra. You don't preach your dogma, and I won't preach my catma."

The sun grew fiercer as noon approached and they sped across the border to Myrtle Beach. MapQuest led them to their oceanside hotel, a squat, lime-green tower, at least ten stories high, with a sandy lobby. She rushed to their room and yanked open the drapes. Her heart sank.

"What's this crane doing there?" A huge industrial derrick blocked their view, abandoned in some mysterious effort of beachfront construction.

Neal laughed. "Just my luck. I bet we have the only room on the strip without a view."

"God, you're such a pessimist."

Freda ran downstairs to the front desk, but all other rooms were booked.

When she came back, he said, "We'll be at the beach the whole time anyway."

"God, I'm so pissed!" Things felt stalled today, off balance. She moped until Neal convinced her to go to the beach.

"Let's drive down the strip to the public access area," he said. "I promise there will be no cranes."

On the way Neal cussed out anyone who drove like it was Sunday, which seemed to be all drivers. Finally Freda snapped, "Stop polluting my air!"

Neal said, "Get these mouth breathers off the road, then."

She almost said, *We're fighting like an old married couple.* She felt herself twitch like a cat wanting to bolt.

Neal found the last space in the public lot, next to a large blue van. Freda snickered when she saw the name painted on the side. "The Blue Licks Assembly of Precious Redeeming Blood," she announced. "That's almost as bad as, I don't know, Lizard Lick Loves the Lord."

She almost got him laughing. But he seemed overly serious as he said, "Blue Licks is an actual place in Kentucky."

"Okay, fine, Lizard Lick's for real, too, but that doesn't excuse 'Precious Redeeming Blood.'"

"It's language some people use in worship."

"Well, it's lame—a turn-off."

"I doubt you're the target audience."

"Pardon me for having an opinion!"

They walked to the beach and found a spot with an unsullied view of the water. Neal peeled off his shirt and headed into the waves. Freda settled on her towel and pulled out *The Kite Runner*.

The sun blanketed her and the breeze lapped at her skin. She felt safe and still: a strange, rare feeling. She watched Neal dive, resurface, and dive again, buffeted by the surging tide, happy like a kid. She remembered how quiet and centered she felt when they had first met, how everything slowed to a crawl while they talked for hours. She always remembered that café date with their heads close together, his hazel eyes inches from hers and lit with interest. Yoga, Frida Kahlo, Merlefest, sushi: they loved the same things. They swapped books every few days, and Neal devoured everything she gave him, including all the used books she'd bought but never read. Neither cared about cars or clothes, and they both earned less than a living wage so they could pursue their passion—or in her case, find one. On the differences side, there was religion, and the animals thing. She would never, ever call herself a Christian and he would never own a cat. She felt sure he just hadn't met the right feline yet.

She opened her eyes when she heard shouts and cackles. A family stood directly in front of her, dumping gear and snapping out towels. All this beach and they needed to roost right here? The patriarch wore a Confederate flag do-rag wrapped around his head and carried a pregnant gut. He dropped a huge cooler with a grunt. His wife with fried blond hair balanced a cigarette on her lip, dragging a Confederate flag boogie board. She plopped on a towel with her *Star* magazine. The man snorted like a bear as he rooted through the ice and cracked open a Bud Light. The teen boy, his concave chest already lobster-red, darted down the beach hollering, "Somebody throw me the damn ball!" His tow-headed preteen sister, her belly straining against a hot-pink swimsuit, wandered squinting down the beach, dangling a catcher's mitt. The ball sped by her every time he threw it. Now one stranger, then another, now a third was forced to retrieve the ball when it rolled onto their towels. The father ambled in a circle around the cooler, watching the waves as he sipped his Bud and rotated his Hulk Hogan shoulders.

When Neal came back dripping, he found Freda seething—her brow furrowed and not a page turned in her book. He wondered what could be wrong now.

"There's no forgiving white trash," she spat, barely under her breath.

Neal watched their neighbors for a long minute. "I was a country-ass kid like that," he murmured.

"Come on, you weren't trailer trash."

"I'd never seen the ocean. Me and my brother, I guess I was six or seven, we acted like a bunch of yard apes." He gave the group another look. "They're about as ugly as homemade sin."

She laughed. He warmed at the success of his humor—often it could lift her out of her moods—and opened his book. But she refused to look away, could not stop burning holes in the backs of this crew and its train wreck—"trailer wreck," Neal thought, then decided it didn't play—and would not stop twitching beside him, sighing and glaring. He knew if she watched any longer, she might yell something she regretted. So he wasn't surprised when she threw her book and sunglasses aside and, giving the family a wide berth, ran toward the water.

Neal watched her head into the tide, her strong legs and broad shoulders plowing the water like a dolphin, shining hair sleek and black, the gods of the sea embracing her. He wanted to take her in his arms again, calm her down, and most of all savor this rare time away from her hovering friends. Nearly all their dates lately had become group outings, nonstop chatter about grassroots politics, vegan recipes, and indie music. Her friends were pleasant to him, but their looks of idle if not invasive curiosity left him feeling caged. They all seemed to wonder at this Christian, teetotaling yet supposedly literary boyfriend Freda tolerated—an improbable aberration from her normal love interests.

He watched her swim back and forth and then tread water a long while, her eyes fixed on something. It was a black family—mom, dad, boy, and girl—walking slowly near the water's edge. He knew she was imagining their discomfort passing near the family with the Confederate flag gear. Freda was tender to the point of heartbreak for any cause you could name. He called her girlfriends "Freda's Fretters" since together they stewed over all the world's wrongs—election fraud, African genocide, global warming—as if anxiety would somehow speed the salvation of the planet. Their worry seemed like a huge, amorphous albatross beyond hope or relief.

When she returned, she seemed calmer. The family she found so heinous had wandered down to the water, their voices muted by the roar of the ocean. She lay down on the towel, became flat and still, and went to sleep.

The humid heat and beating sun sat on everything like a weight. Freda woke a while later to blink at Neal, still reading. His collection of Flannery O'Connor stories sat propped on his wet stomach, swelling with dampness, the cover cracking from repeated exposure to sun and surf, now a mosaic of sand-studded patches. She watched him methodically read and reread the same story three times. Freda planned to borrow the book after she finished *The Kite Runner* and Deepak Chopra. Or maybe he'd loan it to her so she could read just a story or two, since she could never finish anything. She was too interested in too many things—a blessing and a curse. She dozed and woke, then dozed again, loving how the heat stifled her to quiet where only her mind could wander sluggishly. She spun a fantasy of their life together someday in an Asheville bungalow. Here was the porch and the hammock; there, the composted garden with basil, rosemary, and tomatoes. Two cats from a shelter chased bugs through flowers. On that hammock, she would read her unfinished stacks of books. Inside the bungalow she would learn to knit and make stained glass. He would write on the porch with that furrowed brow, ravenous to find the right words but no longer snappish, free from his dead-end job to pursue his art. She would not work anywhere if she could: she'd had enough of her two odd jobs: arts council receptionist and receptionist at a massage therapy studio. Maybe by Asheville she'd have her massage license or an MFA or something.

She considered his narrow eyes and the catlike V of his jaw. Even the shape of him was hunger, like his lust after words and what he deemed to be capital-T truth. The way he held her at night, as if she were something precious, made her feel she was some of the Eden he sought.

She woke again to the sound of Guns N' Roses blasting from the family's boom box. They squatted around their cooler, shoving one another and squalling about supper—a Bojangles' one, from the looks of the bags. Since there was no sign of the tumult letting up, Freda stood. She started slinging books and towels into their totes, scattering sand she hoped would sting the trailer trash. Neal followed her to the parking lot.

"Uh, would you like to tell me where we're going?" Neal called.

"Jesus Christ, the torture's finally over," Freda said with a sigh. "Can we please get something to eat?"

In the parking lot as they loaded their car and rinsed their feet in the outdoor shower, they heard a commotion behind them—that family, tumbling toward the Blue Licks Van. Neal and Freda backed away from the shower and waited inside the Subaru for them to trundle away. "If you try to pull out now, you might hit one of them," Freda muttered under her breath. "These people are so *unconscious*."

Neal said, "Yeah, they're something else."

The van fired up with a muffler loud as a rocket launcher, and tires shrieked as the van backed up fast and tore out of the lot.

"If that's what the children of God look like," Freda said, "who the hell wants heaven?"

Neal felt blood beating in his head. Why she always had

to cut on Christians—why she couldn't ever let anything go because there was always some religious conspiracy afoot—he couldn't really understand. "Get off your high horse," he snapped. Then he saw her face and regretted his temper. "I mean: I wish you wouldn't take that tone."

"What tone? You snapped at me."

"You were being...nasty."

"Nasty? How? Why do you always censor me?"

Neal sighed as he started the ignition.

"This is just like Deer Ridge," she said, fuming. "Always telling me what I can and can't say."

"You could have let it go—"

"The guy's up on stage making racist comments and I'm supposed to stay silent?"

"He was an idiot fresh out of prison. No one listened to him." But she was no longer listening either, so he backed the car out of the space and pulled out of the lot.

They drove in silence, Neal hating the quiet, wanting to make it stop. Every day, they fought like this—sometimes twice or three times a day now. Why did that bonehead mandolin player at the Deer Ridge Bluegrass Festival have to make that stupid comment, "Sure is good to see some white people"? It drew a big laugh from the redneck crowd, but Freda got so fired up she complained to the festival organizers and wrote a letter to *Freedom Weekly.* Then she walked away from another performance when a singer dedicated his song to the unsaved.

"Black gospel's all about salvation, and yet you love that," Neal had argued with her in the festival parking lot as she stalked around their car, threatening departure. "Can you please tell me, what's the difference?" Though Neal already knew: the gospel singer was an old white man with a pompadour.

She couldn't explain and refused to stay, so they left the festival early.

Remembering that moment made him mad all over again as he turned onto Highway 17, the main drag that Neal liked to call Redneck Vegas: that strip where all the temptations of the flesh drew those with dulled senses. Where one could stop at Vices Smokes 'n' Liquor for a quick fix, or better yet, the local gas station for a Lottery/Smokers Drive Thru; where the Bottoms Up Gentleman's Club offered sensual pleasure in what looked like an abandoned warehouse; where a billboard beckoned with promises of shellfish delights—*I Got Crabs at Dirty Dick's!*

"Redneck Vegas," he said, hoping this joke would ease the tension, "where fools come to—"

"Where racists come to lynch African-Americans," Freda finished for him.

"Let me ask you something," he said. "Do you have any black friends?"

"What does that matter?" She stared down the road as if she were willing him and everything else away.

"Every day you talk about racism this and racism that. Did you play football and basketball with dudes from the 'hood? Did you survive the riots during busing? Have you worked landscaping, construction, trucking? Guess who has. White boy here. Every Sunday night I stand next to Evelyn and Grover who run our soup kitchen at the church. They're veterans of the Movement. I know me some black people, mos def."

"Well, gold star for you." She folded her arms and turned to the window. "And don't mimic the way they talk. That's racist."

They drove a few miles down the strip. He had no idea where they were going, so he had to say, "Where to?"

"I don't care!"

He suddenly felt so hungry he could eat an entire seafood buffet. He chose Boo's Biscuit Shack, within their budget and just a few icy minutes away.

When she got out of the car, he heard her gasp.

"Goddammit!"

"What?" he said, heart thundering.

"That damn Blue Licks van!" Freda hollered. She pointed at a long scar on the right side of Neal's Subaru, scraped down to the metal. "Damn white trash! I'm calling the police."

"Aw, man," Neal said with a groan. He squatted to inspect the damage. It looked like slightly more than his deductible. On a ten-year-old car, definitely not worth the trouble.

He slammed his door. "I don't care. Let's get dinner; I'm starving."

"No, damn those assholes!" She pulled out her phone, but hesitated; he could see her mind weighing whether this was a decent use of 911. "We should call your insurance—where's your card?"

He handed it over, reluctantly.

She punched in the number and listened, frowning. "Shit, shit, shit! I'm out of minutes!"

"Don't worry about it. I'll mess with it later." He couldn't offer his own pre-paid phone, empty of minutes as well, because his credit card was maxed for this trip and his checking account, close to empty.

She thrust the card back at him and got in the car, fuming. He knew the bulk of her anger stemmed from him not taking charge the way she wanted. That and his lack of a phone with unlimited minutes.

Their food at the Biscuit Shack took forever, and even

though the greasy-good meal of a meat and three sides filled them up, she couldn't stop recounting the incident and plotting how no-count people without insurance could be forced to pay what they owed.

"You can't prove they did it," Neal said.

"Who the hell else could it be? They were parked right next to us!"

She insisted they go back to the parking lot at the beach and look for them.

There in the lot was the van, its crew spilling out in the fading sun with soft-serve cones and boogie boards.

Freda jumped out of the car and raced over, calling, "Hello, excuse me! You scraped our car!"

"Like he-e-ell we did," cried the teen.

Neal hustled over. "Hi, I'm Neal," he began, but Freda interrupted, "Yes, you did. We need to call the police."

His father grunted, breathing like a hard sleeper, his hand on his pocket. The teen snarled, "Ain't gonna be no po-po here."

"Po-po?" Freda snapped. "The Confederate flag everywhere, and you talk black?"

The father said, "Don't you talk about my son." He sprang open a large knife.

"Whoa, now," Neal said.

"Aw, Randy," whined his wife, "not this shit again."

Freda and Neal backed away to the tune of the family's laughter. "Peace out, assholes!" screamed the young girl, her sweaty face pink as her swimsuit.

Inside the car, doors locked, Freda scrambled for her cell, trembling so hard she dialed 991. Behind them they heard a roar and squeal of tires, then saw a blue blur as the van lumbered off.

"Wow. That was stupid," Neal said. Then he cackled. In

the cool after the explosion, despite his heart thundering so hard it filled his ears, everything seemed funny.

Freda yelled, "No, that was *cowardice!*" Now she could dial 911.

Neal felt himself turning red. If she was calling him a coward...hell, he could have whupped Do-Rag's ass if the guy hadn't been armed. What did she want—a bloody throw-down? Him landing in the hospital?

He closed his eyes and breathed words his sponsor recommended: *Serenity. Acceptance. Peace.*

"They should be locked up!" yelled Freda. The operator answered, and Freda had to repeat "Blue Licks Assembly of Precious Redeeming Blood" three times while Neal laughed himself silly. The operator asked them to stay at the scene until an officer arrived. They waited an hour and no one came.

"They probably stole that van," Neal said.

They rode in silence back to the hotel.

"Look," Neal said when they entered their room. "The crane's gone."

She wouldn't look. She said, coldly, "I want to go home."

When she was in this mood, she wouldn't snap out of it until she was ready. He'd learned the hard way. He stood at the window, taking in the unsullied view. *Serenity. Acceptance. Peace.*

He turned, and she was curled in an angry fetal ball on the bed. "I'll check out then," he said. He left the room.

In the car driving back to Chapel Hill, she buried her nose in *The Kite Runner.* Gradually she felt the weight on her chest lift. After an hour, she looked up, ready to talk. "I need a bookmark," she said.

"There's one in the Flannery," he said.

She reached over the back seat and got in the tote

holding the books. She pulled out the story collection and found a grocery receipt inside with Neal's tiny, tight scrawl marching across it like ants. It was a list with a title: *The Liberal Decree.*

White people, bad. Black people, good.

Bluegrass gospel, bad. Black gospel, good.

Straight people, bad. Gay people, good.

Fox News, bad. NPR, good.

U.S.A., bad. Any other country, good.

Western religion, bad. Eastern religion, good.

"What the hell is this?" she said.

He glanced down. He turned slightly pink.

"Notes for a story," he said.

For a moment she didn't breathe, feeling the dream of it all, but the next moment she was back in her body, still staring at her whole self reduced to flat labels. Like preservatives, chemicals, high-fructose corn syrup—all the things she wasn't. Yet him, he wanted her to live in saccharine la-la land—the fake Wonder Bread world of conservatism and heavenly salvation.

He could have it.

"Freda," he said after a minute, "Please don't take it the wrong way. It's just something I'm working out in my head."

She said nothing. He waited a few more minutes.

"So you're not going to talk?" he said. "Can we at least discuss this?"

"You've made your decision," she said.

"About what?"

"About who I am."

"That's not true."

She shook the receipt in his face, and he flinched. "It's here in black and white!"

He had no idea what to say. Though he knew it was futile,

he played Mahalia Jackson, The Roots, and Zap Mama, her favorites, the rest of the way home.

When they entered Chapel Hill, he didn't ask her to stay over. Instead, he drove straight to the bungalow she shared with three other women and its yard full of sunflowers and rusting art, including a banjo man made of hubcaps and axles.

Her heart sank; he wasn't even going to fight for her and ask if she wanted to stay over. He would rather spend the night with his Bible.

He cut the engine and turned to face her. "Freda," he said. "I'm so sorry. Please forgive me. That list was stupid. I was irritated one day, and I just wrote that out. I totally forgot about it. You saw a page out of my head and it should be burned."

Something inside her fluttered, wanting to forgive him. But then again, he'd had these thoughts, such ugly thoughts— never mind his thinking this apology would suffice.

"Don't worry," she said, and he looked hopeful. "Anytime you want, use the bleeding-heart liberal for material. Hell, why don't you put me in The Never-Ending Novel."

His pale blue eyes stared. That was nasty, and she knew it. Ten years he'd spent slaving over the thing and still nothing to show except two hundred pages, a pile of rejection slips, and a daily gig at Right Price books where he shelved paperbacks crumbling with mold and dust.

She got out of the car, pulled her things out of the trunk, and walked up the gravel driveway choked with weeds. He backed out too fast, tires squealing and gravel flying.

Inside he felt tremors, an itching of the soul. They had crossed some invisible, high-voltage line. How comforting it would be right now to head downtown to the sideshows of The Pit or The Empty Glass and shred Freda's name with a beer in hand. Flirt with some sloe-eyed girl, and spin a yarn for anyone who would listen. For a second he felt the hard yearning on his tongue, the pull toward lazy hours with fellow anti-heroes, characters with no plot, singing the "I'm gonna do this and that" refrain. Then he saw himself tomorrow morning, splayed out in his bed with a vicious headache, paralyzed with self-hate and a coated tongue. Back where he started—stuck, fifteen again, passed out on the floor of another party. Never to age, evolve, change.

The longing passed.

His AA sponsor had asked him when he started dating Freda if her barhopping was a problem. Neal had told him no, because Freda didn't really drink; she went to bars to be social. At least places she chose were a step up from his old haunts: Obscura and Veritable Vino gathered drunks with day jobs and steady incomes. And they never stayed long because she couldn't stand sitting still.

He turned on the TV and watched ESPN, sipping from a liter of Canada Dry. The bubbles made him feel he was getting something out of nothing. In bed that night he read the gospel of John again, trying to rouse a thrill of comfort, but words saying he should be in the world but not of it left his mouth dry as dust. He wondered where Freda was out in that world and what guys were keeping her of it, in it, all about it. He tried to see a future with her ten years from now, her still stopping by bars, still dead set against organized religion, still wiser than he about black people. It would be a story full of restless yet static action.

The next afternoon, when Freda got home from the massage studio, she had a message. It was Neal asking her to call him, his voice low and dull, overshadowed by the chatter of Right Price customers and the cash register. Maybe he'd repented his rant—maybe that horrible list was a conservative's last stand, the final privately staged rebellion. It wasn't like he'd read it to her. God knows she'd whined enough to her girlfriends about his Bible obsession and his right-wing politics, and she desperately needed that sacred space to say her piece. Neal was old school, without male friends who might listen with some sensitivity, nor did he keep a coterie of good female friends because he insisted men and women couldn't be friends. He had nothing but his writing.

Sometimes a person needed to blow off steam, especially when they were on the cusp of change. She had tried so hard to help him see how gray everything truly was.

Now she regretted not saying goodbye yesterday. She felt lighter, having this feeling, as if the road before her no longer kinked and twisted. She and Neal would reconcile. They always did. She could refrain from anti-religion comments if he could ease up on his judgments. To be fair, he never quoted Scripture at her. If he could just lose the love affair with a text boasting four hundred versions...How could it be anything but metaphor?

When she called him around ten, she kept her voice light and happy. "Hey, sweetie! Guess what?"

"What?" His voice was sad, but it wasn't a wall.

She said, "Pluto's not a planet anymore. Scientists say it's just space junk."

A pause. Then he said, "One day it's a planet, the next day it's a ball of ice."

"So much for science!" Freda heard her voice like someone else's, a bit too shrill. "Some things are *eternal*. You don't budge the stars—they can't just cross it out! Pluto's about transformation, about moving beyond the ego!" Maybe he would get her metaphor. He loved metaphors. They both needed a big dose of Plutonic wisdom right about now.

"I guess it's just not big enough."

"That's so male: size always matters!"

He didn't laugh.

"Neal, I'm joking."

"Freda. Listen. You're probably thinking what I'm thinking. It's—it's just not working." Quiet. Then: "We should end things."

She heard her heart beat in her chest, then her throat, now her head. "So this is how you do it," she said. "Over the phone."

"I wish we were happier."

More quiet.

He said, sounding nervous, "Am I not right about that?"

"Sure. Whatever." He just didn't want to make the effort. That was the only sense she could make of it.

"I'm sorry," he said. "I really like you. But this is too hard."

She said she understood, even though she didn't. She heard herself say goodbye.

She wasn't worth the effort. He'd said as much, a man who'd spent ten years on a novel.

That night she read DivinaTerra's blog post at www. star-seeker.com:

"Pluto symbolizes our deepest impulses that must be brought into the light—or that which must have light brought to it."

Freda wasn't sure what had been illumined except Neal's stubborn religiosity and their incompatibility.

A month later she saw him late one evening at Edge of Reason Café—the same place they'd had their first date. Thirty days since their breakup, here he sat with a tall, lithe redhead beneath the trees at an outdoor table, their hands entwined.

Her hair was smooth as red silk, caught up in a low,

careless chignon. She wore a wooden cross with a twisted strand of silver suggesting Christ's contorted body. They didn't see her as Freda walked by.

So Neal had found himself a hip Christian girl.

Freda found a corner table several feet away beneath the awning and hid behind *Freedom Weekly*. She pretended to read, her chest tight as iron. She hadn't been on a date since Neal broke up with her, though a few male friends, ones she considered brothers, had expressed interest in hooking up. She watched Neal and this girl, despising the elegant lines of her slim legs and the ghostly shoulder peeking from the pale green sweater. So much for the demure Christian girl; she looked like she could quickly shrug it off for a quick roll beneath the café table. Did this one like sitting home watching ESPN and talking Scripture? Maybe she liked living by the Book, to the letter of the law, and didn't mind not thinking for herself. Maybe she was an incarnation from some Victorian dream Neal scrawled on paper and woke one day to find serving him breakfast.

One month. By God, grab a woman, anyone will do, quick, before it gets too scary! It took guts to be alone and face your fears.

Twilight deepened. Freda felt hints of first frost in the air. A barista came outside and turned on the patio heaters.

Neal's face bent closer to this woman's, and now they blurred into the darkness. Freda imagined them speaking the soft words said in the beginning, finding the points of alignment, and sipping from latté bowls giving off the faintest of light.

MIDRIFT

$\int$ OMETIMES LATELY WHEN I STAND up too sudden, my vision gets dark around the edges like a tunnel's creeping in from all sides. It's how they say it is when you have the near-death experience and then rush back from heaven with the light warming your back.

At first I hated being dizzy, but now I don't want to come out of it, same as when your eyes glaze over sometimes, how you see but not see. This psychologist I saw one time on TV said go find that restful place in your head, so I picture me landing some place quiet, like behind Daddy's little shotgun house in Jackson, only fixed up nice, where the paint don't peel and the color is turquoise, bright as those scarab beetles in Monique's books about Egypt. The grass shimmers like angels just dusted it and there's a red, red rose bush, dead center where there used to be scabby lawn full of bald patches. I tell myself, *That rose bush is Mama, blooming away, right out of Daddy's ash heap.*

Lord, I can't afford dizzy today. You got to be on when you take on The Academy. You're staring down brick and stone and columns and miles of flowers, so many I never stop expecting guards with hats like Buckingham.

I pull in the big circle drive and just about run into the stone lion when I see what they got on patrol today: Little Miz Tramp, strutting up the front walk like a ho. Skirt's seven inches above the knee and shirt's two inches above the navel. Somebody get me a ruler. Does this school want Britney Spears sashaying around here? Where is the supervision? She cuts her eyes over here at my Caprice Classic clunking over speed bumps. This thing wants me in real deep debt. I'm going to park this fender-bender right between this silver Audi and that gold Lexus SUV. Every car here got vanity plates in code, like BLKDVA... I don't have time to figure that one out.

I hoof it to the front door, my skin prickling with cold, my midsection wobbling like sweaty Jell-O. Britney and her stomach staple disappeared inside. Damn, already 12:07. This lunch break they give you is hardly enough time to order up heartburn. My ribs grip me like a cage; any breath that's left is locked up tight.

Welcome to Cheshire Prep. Everywhere you look is beige, beige, beige linoleum and white walls, whiter than Whole Foods on a Saturday. Tell me why do the kids get stuck in these Novocain barracks while the admin crib gets the Taj Mahal columns and hardwood floors? They put the pretty part of The Academy up streetside, but inside, you wouldn't think this place cost thirteen G a year. I never can remember where the damn office is. Everything's underground and understood. Now my acid reflux starts to simmer.

A bathroom says "Faculty Women" so I scoot inside, overheated with flashbacks, like what Uncle Franklin used to joke was his Post-Dramatic Mess. I splash water on my face and blink a few times to clear the fog of memories crawling up on me.

I blot my face, put on some lipstick, and suck a shot from my inhaler. That would be my yoga breath for the day. I tell the mirror, "You are looking at the administrative assistant to the CFO of WireTech." That would be my mantra. I check my arms; no soak-through yet on this new silk blouse, praise Jesus. Two-for-one sale at T.J.Maxx. *Put on your shield,* Mama used to say every day; I couldn't look at her, I'd be so mad, but wouldn't you know, she's still right.

I tell her, "My baby's mixed up in some kind of 'disciplinary incident.' This is a first, Mama. Help me."

Mama is somewhere laughing. End of my eighth grade year, I swore to Mama I'd just as soon firebomb Suffolk High as go there. I begged to go live with Daddy in Jackson. He'd only let me come there once, so why I got this dream he'd take me full time, God only knows. At thirteen I was too stupid, thinking I could make those kind of threats and Mama would just forget. I won me an all-expense paid vacation straight to Uncle Franklin's where I sweat out ten pounds picking tobacco all summer. Dripping at sunrise, dripping at supper, grabbing and snapping and tucking leaves all day. Black gum under your nails and in the cracks of your hands. I got nicotine poisoning shoving the leaves up under my arm. I never said another word about Suffolk after that, even though food ran through me like water every damn morning till graduation. Too bad it don't do that now.

I come out the bathroom and right by me goes Li'l Miz Ho, clack-clack-clack on heels, straight into the net of a teacher. Teacher asks her why she's violating dress code. This school's finally cracking down on the rising tide of midriff tees.

Ms. Thang starts her whining but the tall skinny woman with a butch haircut says, "Go change right now or I'll call your mom."

Britney huffs away to get the alleged sweatshirt. Teacher watches her go, making sure she makes it there. Rules is rules, little girl.

If there's one thing you won't catch Monique doing, it's this midriff shit. I haven't smacked her in years but she knows I will if I see her baring and sharing. One time she tried to leave the house in one of those lacy-racy, spaghetti-strap tees, looking like a bony bird poking out that piece of lingerie. We had us a family meeting. Now she covers up with a cardigan, still tight as they come, but she keeps that thing ON. I tell her, "Should I get a call from this school saying someone saw your navel, you know I don't play."

A bell goes "ting," some New-Age sound, and the halls fill up with chatter, and then the swarm comes. An ocean of Abercrombie & Fitch, Lord have mercy. I swim upstream to get at this butch teacher. I holler, "I'm looking for Donna Kennedy."

The woman flashes me a big, horsey smile. "That's me. You must be Antoinette Mabry." Now it'd be real funny if I was like, "Naw, I'm Britney's mama." There's only one bite of chocolate running around the sophomore class.

"Mama!" Someone grabs me from behind, a vise grip. My baby.

I turn around and hold her tight. If Monique's not afraid to hug me in front of God and everyone, then I *know* something's wrong.

"What is going on?"

Monique shakes her head and swipes at her face, fresh wet, her bright eyes crusty. Has she been crying?

Ms. Kennedy points us to a little hallway. We follow.

Monique plops on a chair outside an office door, turned away from the crowd. "Go on, Mama, I'll sit here."

"You sure?"

She swallows hard. I better go before she busts out crying right in front of these people.

Inside Ms. Kennedy's office, her wall says she's a

counselor with degrees from somewhere up north, that she played college ball, and she birthed two Ross Perot babies. She has me sit on a love seat near a box of Kleenex. But she stays standing. "Excuse me just one second," she says, laughing through her words the way nervous white people do.

She's gone just a minute. Then she comes back in and shuts the door, plunking herself in a chair. She's got a man's body, clamping her legs like she don't know how to cross them. "Thanks for coming in. You didn't have to—I wish I had more to tell you, but right now, we're just investigating." She looks at me like I'm so very nice to haul my ass in here. Wouldn't any mama come in at the first word of her child in trouble? "So, I'm sorry to report there's been a cruel prank. Ten girls in the sophomore class received hate letters in their lockers. We believe they were placed early this morning."

I shake my head, suck my teeth. My heart's pounding a drum solo. I say without thinking: "I told y'all to let these kids have locks."

"Trust is part of the Cheshire community mission," Butch says, but she don't look too convinced.

All this stupid kumbaya shit means is people are all up in each other's personal property. "Monique's 'lost,' what, at least five books now? That chemistry book cost near sixty dollars." The scholarship don't pay for that. Tell me why in God's name do *these* kids need to steal? And now we've got a hate crime? I'm telling you what.

Butch looks shell-shocked, so I better calm down and play nice. "Could you please tell me what's in these letters?" I remind myself not to use contractions.

"They're very troubling." Kennedy catches herself looking at her desk. I see a pile of papers with some funky-ass print. These kids got computer access everydamnwhere, so when they blackmail each other they can do it up nice in Macaroni font.

She says, "Basically, the letters threaten each girl, using very personal information, and –"

"Threaten how?" Damn, Antoinette, don't interrupt!

"With—rape, basically."

Say what? "I beg your pardon?"

"Yes, it's very upsetting. We're bringing in a detective. The language *sounds* 'male,'" she holds up long fingers to make quote marks, "but we're not sure it isn't a girl."

My mind's spinning. Number one, ten girls are mixed up in this. That means they can't just put it on Monique. Number two, it may not be a boy. She sure as hell don't need some crazy white boy stalking her; give me a psycho slut any day. It's probably Britney Spears, and Monique can take her.

"We've been searching all the lockers," Kennedy's saying. "But that was after Monique discovered a letter in her locker—on her own, around eight forty-five. She came right to us. So we think the incident occurred some time between eight and eight-thirty, when everyone was in class…"

Monique, what the hell were you doing out of class? She better feel the darts shooting at her from this office. Best not to go to your locker for anydamnthing. That's where the mess always starts, the halls. My daughter's too smart to pull this kind of shit, but this school won't get that news flash. Just waiting for her to mess up.

"I need to see this letter," I say.

Surprise, surprise, she hands it over.

It's typical white girl shit, how Monique's got a fat butt and ugly like a dog. Then, "Bryant and Leon say they've had you twice. That's why I'm going to rape you 10 million times till you die."

Now I know what's got my baby in tears, people saying she lost it to them two. Bryant, he's that one always harassing the only other black male in the class, Leon, telling him he too white, he a prep, when Bryant's black ass been playing tennis his whole damn life up at the club. Just because Bryant listens to that Ludracis shit don't make him ghetto. You should see his Redbone mama with her fancy airs.

Kennedy's going on, "The girls are, understandably, very upset, but we're going to restore our community."

I just give Kennedy a look. Monique's been shivering on her skinny-ass piece of ice with the sharks circling since she started here. How is today any different? I stand up.

"I need to see about my daughter. Please call me if you learn anything new."

"Of course. We're advocating strict consequences, Mrs. Mabry—"

"Ms.," I say. "They don't believe in punishment around here."

She looks all butch and helpless. She knows I speak the truth. That thing last year on the senior class trip where they trashed a hotel in Virginia Beach: all those kids got was a slap on the wrist. Mama and me now, we would have set up a Woodshed Holiday Inn to host their asses, belts and switches. They'd never sit down again.

I open the door and look out, but Monique's not there. "Did you send her to lunch?"

"Yes, I did—"

"Will she come back this way?"

"Yes." Butch looks like she swallowed something nasty. Something is up but I don't know what.

I say goodbye. I've got fifteen minutes till I got to get back to work. Should have had Monique get me something from that cafeteria because otherwise all I got time for is some Nabs, not exactly the Atkins special. I cross the main hall and sit down outside the office to wait on her.

You try to do the right thing. You really do. Monique don't know a lot about how much I worry. Like her going to school with this crew—like this one coming along here, rich loser let's call Mr. Shaggy, can't open his eyes and all grunge with his shirt flapping and laces flopping. Squeals into the parking lot behind us on days I drop Monique off late, in his Jeep with huge antenna, looking coked up some days, stoned others. No one cares about his ass because the parents always in Europe, Monique says. Now here he is lurching into the office to sign in; it's been a liquid lunch if you ask me. A twenty flutters out his sagging britches. A freshman coming in behind, dragging his roller backpack, the Urkel Special, darts to pick it up and give it back, but Shaggy waves him off. I bet he carries around more Gs than my monthly salary. It's all one fine ride downhill.

So on the one hand you got these drug runners and then you got the bulimic debs, girls Monique hangs with. They're like Saran Wrap, nothing to them. Monique says she can hang with anyone, she's friends with all the groups, but what if she's caught up in some Meow Mix I don't know about? These girls, they make a list, and then, they cross you *out*. Death don't come from a kick to the kidneys or someone yanking your weave; it's decision by The Club. It's like they put up a tombstone for you and everyone walks around it. That's how these people do you.

Lord, girl, Mama says over my shoulder, *don't get yourself in a spin. That child's going to be fine. You turned out all right.*

Monique also don't know how I check that grades web

site two, three times a day, just like it's the Dow Jones. Hell, she's my investment. Whenever she says, "Mama, I'll go back to Carthage. Let's get us a house," I say, "Shut your mouth. You're worth more than a mortgage." Never. Not when she's doing so good here, never below a B. This place will get her in a good college. Mama was so proud last fall when Monique made it in after hell freshman year dodging all the trash at Carthage. One posse followed Monique around growling, "Burr burr burr, gonna eat me a skinny girl." Though I had my doubts about Cheshire, and big ones, too. At the time I said to Mama, *Get back to me in June.* It wasn't an easy decision.

Mama, if I'd known how bad off you was, I would have sounded more positive. She had to part with us before Thanksgiving, only one of Monique's grade reports come to us by then. All As and Bs, praise Jesus. I buried it with Mama. Monique don't know that.

I lose my daydream when a loud voice sounding all BBC says, "Well, Antoinette Mabry!"

Thelma Covington, Bryant's mama. Lord, take me now.

"Girl, how you *doing?*" She stands over me, hair the latest Halle Berry, suit one of those Vogue tweedy fringe specials looking like it needs a good hem.

"Just fine!" Look at me squealing back. "How you?"

"*Wonderful!* Listen, did Monique tell you we're having a movie night Saturday?"

"No, she did not. Isn't that nice."

"Well, we sure hope she can come! She's just a gorgeous girl. Stunning!" The woman's got a voice that could kill dogs. While she's gushing, she's halfway inside the office. She flutters a hand with so much ice I'm surprised she can lift it. I'm dismissed. Now she's chatting up the secretary, dropping off some overpriced little plant. I bet she's sniffing out some kind of deal for her son. She knows we're scholarship and while that makes her feel like royalty, she hates it, I can tell. She thinks she's entitled to all the cash. She click-clacks away, singing out, "See you Saturday!", leaving me with a *wink*, Lord Jesus, like we're BFFs.

Make me sick. She and all her other PTA pals thinking they're soul food, slave-history black but meanwhile skating around like White Girls on Ice. That gold Lexus and the license plate. Wait a minute, BLKDVA. Jesus, that was her. Lord, is she for real?

As I was saying. You got the stoners, the debs, and now the cherry on top, the Uncle Toms. Nest of vipers is what it is. You got to ask yourself, what's worse: this place, or where I went? First day of my freshman year at Suffolk, 1982, I see some cracker-ass senior wearing the Confederate flag like a cape. And then that Jewish guy, Horowitz, hollering at me whenever he sees me walking with the only Korean and Mexican on the whole damn campus. He's with the new-money rednecks in their ball caps and Skynrd shirts. Like a megaphone he yells, "Here comes the dog parade!" I holler, "There goes the asshole!" A teacher hears only that part and packs my ass off to ten days' detention.

Then the Suffolk sayonara, Ripley's Believe it or Not, is I had to shake *Jesse Helms'* damn hand at graduation. That racist motherfucker was doing his filibuster on the Dr. King holiday right about that time. Shameful. When he beat Gantt's ass in '90, Mama cried. Three times my whole life I saw her cry, and that was one.

That would be the sum total of my nostalgia for the Suffolk Class of '86.

Kids come through the double doors from lunch, more with roller backpacks; half their asses out of dress code. Finally, here's my baby, carrying nothing but ice cream, one of those Nutty Buddy things. She's swiping at her face still, and I see some dandruff we didn't get, little snow flecks in her chignon she wears all the time now. Never lets her hair down anymore. Rubs her stomach and says it burns sometimes after meals.

"That it for lunch?"

"I'm not hungry, Mama. You want it?"

I take it. She sinks into the seat next to me. I find her a Kleenex. She pulls out her makeup and gets herself fixed.

"Ms. Kennedy says they're going to ask me some questions," she says.

"What's that?"

"They're going to talk to each one of us."

Her shoulders look like two little knobs hunched up. She used to have more meat on her. I say, "You the first to go in?"

"Yeah."

"When?"

"In a few minutes."

She was the first to find the letter; now she's the first to get questioned. The usual suspect...My stomach does a back flip. In 2006 Monique's supposed to graduate this white house, this country club. Might as damn well be 1986.

I stand up and shove the ice cream in my purse. "Your principal—what's his name again?"

"Mr. Millipan."

I stride into the big office. Behind me I hear, "Mama, what you going to do?"

The secretary's a pudge-face woman with kinky gray hair. I know she hates it because it won't bob the way she wants; no lips, either, they're pressed so tight. This one hates her job, too, but hates people most.

"I need to see Mr. Millipan," I say.

"Do you have an appointment?" Won't even look at me, all about her computer screen.

"No, but this concerns an emergency."

She click-click-clicks on her little screen in super slomo. "He can see you at 3:30 tomorrow."

Behind her desk she's got my sign—A LACK OF PREPARATION ON YOUR PART DOES NOT CONSTITUTE AN EMERGENCY ON MINE. Least mine's framed and not tacked up on some lame-ass corkboard.

"He can see me now," I tell her, "before he interrogates my daughter."

Those beady blue eyes read me up and down: *Parent of the Criminal.* Just the way she likes black people. "He'll be available at 3:30 *tomorrow.*"

I turn to a door without a nameplate. "This his office?"

She glares. I knock.

"Excuse me!" Beady Eyes yelps.

"Mama!" Monique calls.

"Come in," says a faint voice. I open the door.

I've seen this man before. Real tall and too skinny, like his pants about to slip off. Thin gray hair and no chin. He's squinting at his computer, and when he sees me, he smiles big like he's real thrilled I'm here.

"May I help you?"

"Mr. Millipan!" Beady Eyes whines right behind me. "I tried to tell her—"

He jumps up, rubbing his hands. "Ah, well, Mrs. Cerban, I'm sure we can work this out."

Mrs. Cerban's purple around the edges. She stomps away.

"I'm Antoinette Mabry, mother of Monique Mabry."

"Rich Millipan." He extends a long, lady-finger hand. I shake it. Moist. "Nice to see you." He shuts us in. This office makes me claustrophobic, crammed full of bookshelves and all these paintings.

I speak over the fear, sounding kind of loud. "My daughter received one of the letters. Can you tell me what this investigation's about?"

"Yes, of course. Please sit down." Another love seat waiting on me; this place's just full of love. He sits down behind his desk and looks curious, like he's so very interested in what I've got to say.

I say, quieter but firm as I can, "I understand my daughter's about to be questioned."

"Yes, we're going to speak with each of the girls." He puts his fingers together like a church steeple.

My heart's about to bust out of my chest. "What kind of questions? Will she be alone?"

Mr. Millipan leans forward, smiling, but I smell me some nerves. "Usually it would be myself and the Dean of Students there."

"Would be or will be?"

He blinks. "Will be."

"Will she have an advocate?" Now that's a gem I pulled out of nowhere.

"You mean her academic adviser?"

Whoever that is. Monique don't talk about it. "A teacher she trusts. Or myself."

"We usually invite the adviser should a student face the Honor Council. But since this is a preliminary investigation, we just need to ask her a few questions."

Come on down to the station, boy. We just need to ask you a few questions. The soundtrack of the streets of South Raleigh me and Mama knew so long. My sweat's damn near destroying this blouse.

"I understand a girl may be the perpetrator," I say. His eyes widen; I bet Butch Kennedy wasn't supposed to let that out. "So I don't want Monique alone when she's questioned.

78

I need your guarantee she won't be accused, being that she was the first to discover a letter and what-have-you." Lord, am I making sense? Do we have any damn rights here?

"This is simply informational questioning, Mrs. Mabry."

"Ms., if you please. There's always going to be a bias, Mr. Millipan. Will she have an advocate?"

"I understand your concern—"

"I've got a few others, too." Damn, chill, girl. I can feel Mama hovering, ready to smack me. "I need to know why Monique has to be the first."

"We like to get right on these things before the students get too stirred up. We—"

"Things is—things are already stirred." Now he's got owl eyes. Righteous anger runs my engine. "I understand you all went through the lockers already."

"Well, Mrs. Mabry," he harrumphs, because he don't handle pit bulls too well, "we are a private institution, as you know, with the right to search if we have cause, such as protecting our students."

"Meanwhile, no one protects the students' property. Monique's lost about $200 worth of books."

We're eyeing each other, and he looks real stupid, deer with no chin caught in headlights. I think he forgot the question. So I say it again.

"I need to know if Monique will have an advocate."

"Well, that really hasn't ever been our procedure—"

"—I think it's time it was."

"Mrs. Mabry, our policy is a result of committee study and faculty approval. I can't reverse our policies on my own. We have a democratic process at Cheshire."

Now that's too funny, but I don't laugh. "What if the policy puts the students in—" I'm hunting for words here "—an unsafe position?" Is "unsafe" in the dictionary?

"Monique will be safe. We value her."

My ass you do. In these kind of investigations, detectives are always looking for the one on the fringe. Sure as hell ain't my baby, wasn't ever me, but who the hell you think they questioned first when a rich white girl named Pinky helped herself to everyone's shit back at Suffolk? Mmm-hmm. *My* black ass.

I take a deep breath. "If you value her so much, give her an advocate."

A small vein's throbbing in his temple. "I understand your position, but there is nothing I can do to change things at this time."

"You're the principal."

The vein jumps like a gymnast. "Mrs. Mabry, I do not appreciate your tone."

"And I don't appreciate this investigation. You can interview her with someone there or I'm taking her home."

Do I mean home for the day? Or home for good? Because I don't know where we go from here.

Little beads of sweat like a pearl mustache on his upper lip as he says, "I don't think things need to go this way." I'm not sure why I make him so nervous; it's not like I hold a wad of Gs over his head.

"I won't have her rights violated like this." I stand up, to place a period right where he can see it.

"Mrs. Mabry, please sit down." He tries to wipe himself off without me seeing, but it's pitiful, it truly is. And then I understand. This is not just a weak man: this is a man with some bleeding-heart *guilt.* It's the Martin King poster on his wall next to the *All Are Welcome Here* rainbow poster for the fags. The gold-letter, hardback copy of *To Kill a Mockingbird* center stage on his bookshelf. Then low on his totem pole is the Harvard diploma, way below eye level, like he's ashamed. He's just the right generation, too, maybe fifteen or twenty years older than me. One of those who sits at home watching the riots every few years, wringing his hands.

We have ourselves a moment of silence while he's stressing.

I help him along. "Do you know why the faculty won't give the students an advocate?"

"I couldn't tell you." Look at him, he's wiped out and relieved to 'fess up. This man could never handle the drugs and guns they got at Carthage; and they call this man the principal.

"Let me ask you this," I say. "Can it *hurt*?"

"I don't suppose it would—"

"—a small thing," I add, my voice soft, "when you think about it."

"It's just a matter of—coordination—"

This right here, this is something for the record books, something for Mama to see. A white man in his fifties intimidated by *me.* If only she had the pleasure.

I say, quiet, "Perhaps just this one time you can have a private-type, you know, arrangement, a kind of exception or what-have-you…maybe a trial run. See how it goes."

His eyes are right with me, a new light shining. I just gave him a hole he can crawl out. He's babbling, "Well, Mrs. Mabry, that's a fine idea. We might just try that."

That's right, I want to say. *It's time you started making some exceptions.* But I can feel Mama shaking her head behind me, breath pushed out like wind.

Mama, come on, now! I've got to get us something here. For all you never had.

He says, "I'm sure Monique's adviser or maybe a particular teacher would be willing to help out…" Note he's leaving me out as an option. But that's all right, that's all right, we've made progress here.

"That sounds just *wonderful*," I tell him. Lord Jesus, I sound bad as Thelma Covington. It's done. Someone's going to be a witness to my baby's interrogation. No one can sub in for Antoinette Mabry, but this individual will be hearing from me before and after, even if we have to rehearse how it's going to go. I bite my tongue to keep from saying thanks. Mama always did, but I make a point not to thank when the thing should be a guarantee.

I say, "May I see the list of questions?"

"I'm afraid not. I hope you understand we need to keep things confidential."

Fine, fine. Let him feel like he won something.

There it goes, that stupid sound they call a bell.

"Can she go find her advocate now?" I like saying the word, it's like sucking on that dark Ghirardelli chocolate. An aftertaste of bittersweet, though. Maybe I barked so loud I scared myself.

"Yes, well, fine, perhaps that's the best idea," he's saying. And just like that, we pull her out of first place. Let someone else blaze the damn trail while Monique gets herself some backup. I nominate Britney. You know her ass is all up in this scandal.

I can see his eyes getting big, his mind starting to turn, all of a sudden hit upside the head with, *What did I just do?* Mister, that's your problem now.

I stand up, smooth my skirt, hold out my hand. He leaps up. We shake. His hand is sopping wet.

"I'm going to get Monique on to class. Please call me tonight and let me know the latest." Meanwhile, I'm so late for work Monique won't be seeing me till after 7:00.

"Will do, will do, Mrs. Mabry. I'm so glad we had this chat."

"Thank you," I say. Damn, that one sneaked out, but I am thankful, Jehovah Jireh thankful, that my baby's left alone. "Goodbye."

I stride by Beady Eyes and out the door. I tell Monique to follow me.

Outside school we sit on a bench. Cold air feels good out here, don't petrify my lungs. I hug her, then keep my hand between her shoulders, firm. Now I'm going to get some answers.

"It wasn't me, Mama."

"Why in Jesus' name would I think it was you?"

"I know, but—"

"Don't you *ever* think I don't trust you." I grab her chin, look her in the eye, then kiss her face hard. "You know what I don't trust. All you got to tell me is why you were in the damn hallway this morning."

"Getting my binder! I couldn't find my English homework, so I had to pull everything out of my locker."

I believe her.

She hunches over again. "I hate this place."

"You didn't yesterday." Yesterday it was nothing but rah-rah this and rah-rah that with the cheerleading squad.

"Well, I hate Jennifer Beech. She's always starting something."

"Britney in the midriff tee, three-inch heels?"

"Yeah."

"Well, baby, let's talk about what you're going to do." I want to say, *Why the hell you hang with Paris Hilton?* But her three years of teenager already schooled me. You get more with honey.

"Lay low," she tells me. "Don't say nuthin'."

That's my baby. We're grinning at each other, because that's our little chant ever since we saw that video by The

83

Roots, good conscious rap, which if you ask me is what we need more of nowadays. "Any idea why she'd do this to y'all?"

"She hate all the rest of us. She pretend she like us, but I was talking to Sara –" now her voice shifts to café au lait, but she don't even hear it, "—and it's like Jennifer's always spreading rumors, and like what, does she think we don't *know*? Like we ain't able to hear in this small-ass school what she up to?" Now she's back, my bilingual baby. "She think she the queen, but—" Monique's cutting her eyes and blowing out her breath all disgusted.

"I know, these people beyond words sometimes. They call it 'leveling.' Dr. Phil talked about it on *Oprah*. Someone jealous of you, they try to bring you down. But Martin King said it best: it's 'the drum major instinct.'"

"Everyone's saying Lanny or Smithson did it."

"Lanny and Smithson? What kind of names—"

"—Mama, get over it."

"Just playing. Hell, I went to school with boys named Winston the Third and BJ, short for Beverly James, so no one needs to lecture me on Freaky-Ass Names for Southern Men. But you sure it's not a boy now?"

"Did you see the letter?" She rolls her eyes, then looks down, embarrassed. "Boys don't talk like that."

"Yeah, I know that's right." The fact that letter mentions the only two black dudes in the sophomore class, you know it had to be a white bitch writing that shit. It's too obvious, and I'm stupid to think anything else.

"Or you know what?" Monique's saying, this thoughtful look on her face, "I bet it's *Emily*."

Emily's that little mousy thing who is as fringe as fringe can get. Her parents are some kind of trust-fund, sprout-eating hippies who adopted her. She's mixed, the sad kind, with that wide yellow nose and nappy hair.

"Yeah, she wishes she was Jennifer. She's like *obsessed*." Monique's sigh is deep. And I see all of a sudden that Jennifer's the easy target. That diva don't look smart enough to do much more than run her mouth and strut her stuff. It's the fringe kid who feels it raw like a blade to the gut, to where she hates everyone as much as I did. Yes, the outsider can think up some sick-ass shit in all their spare time and maybe even write it down.

It'll take the detective ten days when it takes my baby less than ten minutes. I can see she's worrying on Emily; damn the weight of this anorexic, strung-out school. *Mama, if she can just keep on keepin' on...*

The cold gets to us a little, so I put my arm around her.

"What class you supposed to be in right now?"

"Ms. Droite's."

"She the one that teach you how you oppressed?"

"No, Mama! Ms. D's my history teacher." Monique's got some English teacher who can wrap her lips around the word "oppression." What was it that woman told her, something about so many systems of oppression—the race thing, class thing, and the gender thing—that black women got to deal with. I think they were studying *Raisin in the Sun*. Anyway, didn't nobody bring that shit up when I was in school. We come a long way, baby; now we talk in big SAT words about the hate still around.

"Girl, you need to get to class and I've got to beg my job back." She looks mad for some reason, so I grab her hand. "Baby, I don't have much wisdom except a high school diploma. I don't have the college degree to swear to you it's all worth it, but you're going to do better than me. Of course now, I had you, best thing I ever did, and you know how proud I am. Now if it gets too hateful here, then we pull you out. End of story. But if you think you can hang in, well..." I sometimes wish she'll say, *Get me out of here.* I'd love to see her do what I never got to do, turn her back on these people for good. Then we could buy what we have my eye on; the little blue-and-white house on the cul-de-sac that's two story with a big back yard and a door blue as Caribbean sky...

Monique's eyes got the old look back. "Hey, Mama, think about it: White girls got the letter, too. It's an equal-opportunity institution." She giggles.

"That's all there is here," I grump at her, "white chicks showing skin."

"You know what I mean."

"I know. You in The Club now." I look at her, hard. "Don't you lose yourself, you hear me?"

"*Mama*, I *hear you*." Then she looks solemn, like she's already graduated the school of life. "It's like one of those foreign exchange programs." Now she gets her voice going half-Valley Girl. "Like, don't I, like, fit in, like *seriously?*" She's a mess.

But I don't laugh, and she looks spooked. "Mama, come on, it'll be fine." She wants to please me so bad it hurts. Now I got to make her laugh.

"Britney, she gon' get preg," I say. I'm hoping she'll pick up the joke we have about the fools on court TV, always showing their dirty laundry. *Just like the world want to see niggers*, Mama used to say.

"She already been preg—an' drunk," Monique says, giggling.

"I got preg," I say, punching her shoulder, "and a good thing that was, too."

"But you wadn't drunk," Monique says, and she's grinning more.

"Naw, naw," I say, but I can't look at her. Truth is I always was, back at college, which is why my business never got finished there. Monique, she don't get that choice. "Now I just scored you an advocate, so drag Ms. Trot's liberator ass into that meeting, hear me? You say she's got your back, for real?"

"It's Ms. Dro-o-ttt." She purrs out French r's, looking frustrated, I don't know why. "She's cool, Mama."

"All right then. That who you going to pick?"

"I don't know. I mean, I'll think of somebody."

"This is special. Meaning, you the only one that gets one. So you know what that means."

"—Don't say nuthin'." Now I hear a parrot, not my baby girl. She won't look at me. Maybe she's guessed the rules of this game, the slippery slope up. Well, precious girl, it's a little ugly when you look too close, but the point is, we're making it.

"All right then." I've got to go. I dig for my keys, come up with the Nutty Buddy, all soft. My purse is a mess of vanilla and chocolate. "Give me a kiss."

"Mama," she says.

I'm wiping off my hands. "What?"

"I can do it. I can handle it."

"I know you can."

"Like, I mean alone. It'll be fine." She stands up, smiling through some kind of scared.

"Monique," I say. My throat clogs. "What did you say?"

"Bye, Mama."

She darts at my face and her lips smack my cheek. Just as quick, she's backing off, fast as she can go. She's in that door, and she's gone.

I see how she planned it like this: drop the bomb and then run. After all I...

Well now.

Doing things her own damn way and no other. You try and stop her. Just like me.

The breeze cuts into me, cooling my sweat. Mama's right above, laughing her way through a rendition of "Too Close to Heaven." I know down deep my baby's a strong sapling, the start of an acacia tree, the kind where the trunk don't bend or bow. She's planted in somebody's brand-new garden I don't recognize. Some of her branches stray just like her mama, but that's all right, that's all right. Sometimes you got to get a little lost on the way to being free.

SERENDIPITY

IN THE BEGINNING, THE IDEA came from a bag of chips—Crunchettos, to be exact—owned by an eighth-grader—thirteen-year-old Franklin Crick, to be proprietary. This was how Andy Swindon, middle-school science teacher and two-time finalist for Teacher of the Year, stumbled upon his most innovative unit yet. It was the second month of his seventh year of teaching, early October with leaves flushing electric orange outside the classroom window, when the idea, like the first of several balls sliding down a smooth silver chute in his head, clicked into place.

It began when the last bell rang ending seventh period, when Franklin announced to the class he would be shaving his head at 4:15 that day.

"You're a freak, man," Jimmy Jones said, and thumped Franklin so hard on the back he lurched forward several feet. Then Jimmy scooted out of the room as fast as his football player mass would let him.

Andy realized after five seconds he should stop Jimmy. When he got to the door, the halls swarmed with students shrieking and slamming lockers so hard the air shook. He turned away from these sounds and smells, which were like daggers to his head. What was it he was about to do? Check on Franklin.

Franklin stood in the empty room with his back to Andy, head pressed against the window, watching students rush the buses below. This body language could mean sadness or fear.

Andy said, "It's safe now."

Franklin turned, his face blank as rock. He lifted a Crunchettos bag and yelled, "We have to go to the computer lab, *now!*"

"Okay," Andy said. "Let me get my hand sanitizer."

The halls were clear. The lab was also empty of students, and the lab supervisor. Franklin found a computer, and while Andy scrubbed his hands with thirteen vigorous rubs, Franklin launched Google. Franklin pulled up www.crunchettosexplosion.com.

They watched a white screen and hourglass icon while the computer blinked and made grinding noises as if clearing its throat. Andy counted sixty-seven ceiling tiles and two hundred twenty-three bricks in this room.

Franklin thumped amphetamine drum rolls on the computer table. He cracked his neck and knuckles. Andy wanted to join in but sat on his hands.

Finally, the site loaded, the screen turned black, and a red-and-yellow Crunchettos bag danced for them on its corners, springing joyfully left, right, and center.

Franklin waved his bag in front of the popcorning icon, but nothing happened.

"These machines suck!" Franklin yelled. "It won't show the video!"

Andy said, "We may need to update the Flash settings."

Franklin's black boot jackhammered the floor and he grimaced, biting his lip so hard Andy wondered if there would be blood.

The machine stopped grinding. "Try again," Andy said. Franklin waved the bag.

Red letters appeared below the icon: *Rotate bag.* Franklin

waved the bag in slow motion, aligning the bar code with the message. The screen went black, then two names blinked: OCD Clown and Real Talk Nation.

"OCD Clown!" Franklin said, clicking the mouse. "Real Talk sucks."

"What's OCD Clown?"

"Duh! The best band ever!"

The sound of a cheering crowd chanting, "OCD, OCD, OCD!" swelled as the screen went black. A bassist, lead guitarist, and drummer appeared—each image its own distinct piece of video, as if clipped from a movie like a paper doll. The guitarists tuned their instruments and the drummer tossed his long hair while the invisible crowd roared. Franklin rotated the bag right, and the figures grew in size; left, and they shrank to dots. He moved the bag up and they jumped; down, and the musicians' feet slammed the stage. The band played fast and unfazed while Franklin swept bodies in every direction. Andy caught a lyric, *I hate it when she's not around*, something about a guy in love with a girl who always kept him waiting.

Franklin popped his jaw four times, a tic Andy knew meant excitement, and handed Andy the bag. "Kill it!"

Andy crushed the bag, and the entire stage crumbled. A huge grin split Franklin's face. Then the computer froze.

Franklin smashed his fist on the table. "No!"

"Wait a minute," Andy said.

They gave it a whole two minutes, Franklin jittering nonstop. Then he sprang from the chair, eyes on the floor. "I'm gone." He ran out, leaving his Crunchettos bag uncrumpling like a strange flower.

With Franklin gone, ideas swarmed Andy like bees. What if his students could manipulate avatars in science class? Inhabit a 3-D virtual world to conduct an experiment and solve a problem?

He Googled this Crunchettos technology, heart accelerating. This "augmented reality" merged 3-D, video, webcams, and interactivity. If only he could duplicate this without a fleet of programmers and grant funding. He Googled "simulation + augmented reality." Up popped a pilot program sponsored by Jannus Technology Institute and free to public schools: Save Spring Valley, a simulation named for Rachel Carson's *Silent Spring* where people and animals mysteriously sickened. Using avatars, kids could fly, swim, and jump throughout the valley like superhero EPA sleuths. They would take water samples, eavesdrop on sick residents, form hypotheses, and design experiments to find the cause. This was it—the perfect simulation for his microbiology unit! He could be the first of this small town, perhaps the entire state of West Virginia, to push science teaching into the twenty-first century! The ball, a perfect sphere, slid down the chute: click!

That Eureka he desperately craved had come; no longer would he chew his nails down to blood searching for pedagogical perfection. He must be better than best, especially while his wife stayed out late every night directing the high school play. Fear infected the air when Elsa was unavailable to soothe his panics. But when she heard this idea, she would smile with that crooked little front tooth and soft, pink lips; she would wrap her skinny arms around him; and all would be well.

This could be the lesson to engage Franklin. It could be the lesson that moved his grade from F to D; it might just get Franklin graduated and into high school, where Elsa could then take care of him. Andy had not yet found a lesson that worked, and Elsa had told him many times Franklin would probably be his biggest challenge this year. "Teach every day to your lost soul," she insisted. Lost kids were her specialty. She was right, because today's microbes lesson, one of Andy's best, had proven utterly ineffective with Franklin, who spent the whole class playing a game on his phone. Something else had to work.

Andy stood and counted computers in the lab: thirty-five, but only twenty-seven dependable; twenty-five with a working mouse; and only one reliable printer. If twenty-nine students in seventh paired up, it would be possible to stage Save Spring Valley here.

Andy drove home excited as a kid, tapping out prime rhythms of three, five, and seven on his cracked steering wheel. Through winding mountain roads to their dark brown split level, awaiting him like a safe cave tucked into the hillside, he counted NRA and Palin bumper stickers until he reached twenty-nine, his age and a beautiful prime. Twenty-nine came naturally; he did not need to force it. He had to tell Elsa this: twenty-nine was what she called "a sign" that he must bring virtual worlds to his classroom. It would be groundbreaking; it would be epic. It would resuscitate an obsolete curriculum and capture Franklin's attention. It would make Elsa smile.

This kind of thinking made his blood race, almost like having sex. It had been twenty days and fourteen hours since he and Elsa had done it. He couldn't wait to tell her his idea. She said his ideas were sexy.

No surprise, she and her skinny little butt weren't home yet. She'd been staying at school past ten most nights since she'd launched rehearsals for *Tootsie*. She and Bryn, her student teacher, had cussed their way through censoring the script so it could be "something this Podunk town can swallow." She'd ranted just this morning about doing *Twelfth Night* instead and making the cross-dressing so homoerotic everyone's Baptist hair would stand on end. "They wouldn't make us censor *that*," she said, "because dumbasses around here have no idea what Shakespeare's saying." When she stalked around the kitchen in her tank top and boy shorts, flushed red and fuming, Andy wanted to grab her and maul her the way he hugged his big teddy as a child of eight, nine, and ten, until his mother threw it away.

It was 4:43 p.m. in an empty house. There was nothing to do but make himself his Monday dinner: Smucker's grape jelly on Wonder Bread and Lay's plain potato chips. He would never eat a corn-based product such as Crunchettos even though Franklin claimed they were "the best ever." Andy only believed in what his father joked were The Five Food Groups: grape jelly, plain potato chips, fish sticks, white bread, and applesauce. Just the right levels of neutral smell and cushy softness.

During dinner he watched the ticker on ESPN. When stats began to repeat, he surfed the Save Spring Valley web site on his iTouch, committing key text to memory, then sent an e-mail to the project coordinator, asking if Troy Middle School could join the pilot.

Throughout the evening he checked Facebook. Sometimes it was a better gauge what his wife was up to than anything else. She hadn't posted anything in twelve hours, not since the status update of TOOTSIE'S THE BOMB LOL LMK R U COMING. Some sort of dare with her acting students, she said, to see how much "ridonkulous netspeak" you could cram into one post. Beneath that a student with a profile picture of a big wet pink tongue plus ring posted: LMFAO. Andy would need to ask her what that meant.

Franklin had posted a shot of his new look—a head shaved smooth, making his elfin face even more narrow and feminine. Tomorrow part of Andy's job would include stopping the fag comments. He was getting better at predicting student behavior since Elsa told him the kids at Troy Middle thought diversity was refried beans from Wal-Mart. The school was ninety-seven percent white, jaundiced and spindly from a diet of chicken nuggets and Mountain Dew, followed by less than one percent African-American, rounded off by an occasional and transient sprinkling of two percent Indian or Latin-American, imported by Flora Chemical, the only local corporation besides chain stores and restaurants.

Andy's iTouch pinged. It was the project coordinator of Save Spring Valley, e-mailing him back with a "Welcome!" subject line. Andy's heart raced again. Ball Number Two: click! This discovery of the simulation via a Crunchettos bag was what some scientists called serendipity. Elsa called this phenomenon many things: karma, kismet, or "a sign." Andy corrected her imprecision, explaining that serendipity was less like magical fate and much more what one should call a "happy accident"—one that allowed the human brain running the experiment to make connections in rational order. He would explain all of this to her again when she came home.

He went into the dining room, which served as their office, and sat at his desktop. His Mac sang with welcome, free of the wheezing that plagued the PCs at school. He logged onto the Spring Valley web site and ran the demos again. He watched the avatars stroll along the riverside and across neon-green terrains affecting water runoff. He observed the log cabins, tanneries, and textile mills. He didn't like the turn-of-the-century prairie garb the avatars wore, nor their somber, horse-like demeanors and jerky movements. The avatars were capable of four expressions: happiness, sadness, agreement, or disagreement. While that seemed like a sufficient range of options, he knew kids would complain this wasn't as cool as *Modern Warfare 2* or *The Sims*. Especially from Franklin, whom he could imagine yelling, "Man, this is *wack*!"

What you could do was collect data such as water samples at the various stations, and you could type dialogue in the text box so teams could communicate during the investigation. He hoped students would find at least four causes for the spread of disease: overcrowding, insect vectors in the swamps, pollution of water runoff to low-lying areas, and limited health care access. This simulation might be the most advanced teaching happening anywhere. He couldn't wait for Elsa to see.

He went to bed around 10:45. Elsa always came in at eleven—sometimes 10:59, sometimes 11:02—but the average could be quoted as eleven. She said being alone on an empty campus didn't scare her. He told her he pictured dark figures with rape in their eyes waiting for her outside the school's theater, but she told him not to think like his comics. So now he turned to what she called his Book of Tricks: counting patches in the crazy quilt and stripes in the wallpaper. Numbers turned a throbbing, racing bloodstream into a trickle of cold marbles, blue as ice.

He woke at 1:03 a.m. and found Elsa asleep, her leg thrown across his as if he were part of the bed. Had she returned later than eleven?

"Elsa," he said, pawing her side. She groaned.

"Elsa," he insisted. "I finally have the lesson for Franklin!"

Her eyes fluttered open for a few seconds; he could see glints of light from the satellite clock reflected there. "Good for you, baby," she mumbled.

"It's augmented reality and there are avatars and the kids will solve a disease outbreak—"

"Sounds like a Breakthrough Kid," she said, words slurring. She patted his arm limply and rolled over to her other side. "Good job."

That was all he needed. She had given her blessing. He slid closer to her and curled his body around hers. Ever since college she had reminded him, "I love taking care of you. If I didn't have you, who would I be?" He buried his nose in the sweet, nutty scent of her skin.

When he woke again at 6:30, Elsa was up and making his latté with honey, soymilk, and the foam right at the rim's edge the way he liked. Anything below he had to hand back. They sat down to talk for the first time in days. Her face was pink—glowing. She looked sixteen with her tousled bangs and bowl cut.

"Baby, we decided last night to put the censored parts back in. Bryn and I will drag these dinosaurs into the twenty-first century!"

"But the play is twentieth century," Andy said. He was tired of Bryn's name. It seemed lately she got too much credit. And he really wanted to talk about how to make sure Franklin became a breakthrough kid. As yet, everything was still hypothesis.

Elsa said, "*Tootsie* was ahead of its time. Not just the cross-dressing but a man getting what it's like to be a woman. People around here need to—"

"Science fiction predicts the future of social issues."

"E-zackly—just like that." She tapped him on the nose, the sign for when he made great leaps in understanding. "Bryn says we have to stop being so conformist and stop editing. She thinks Obama's election is like a sign from God." Elsa chuckled. "You gotta love the idealism of youth."

Andy said, "We're only twenty-nine."

"She's twenty-two, a total baby."

Andy had one eye on CNN's ticker, which was reporting a rise in teen depression and suicide. He lost the train of conversation until he heard Elsa say, "And I got another job!"

"What?"

"Sweets, we need the cash."

Coffee grazed his throat, burning his esophagus. He only made 31K. She made thirty-three, because she taught English and ran the theater program. While she rattled on about the Dollar Store, its easy money, only fifteen hours a week, he folded his hands to stop the tapping Elsa said he should never, ever do. Once he'd tried to explain that the ritual soothed him when he felt flooded by memories of Mom fading nightly into the sofa, slurring insults at his dad—"You can't bring it home, can you?"—but Elsa had shaken her head. "No excuses," she said. "Count inside your head or something." Then her mouth did a strange twist, and she added, "I think your mom meant something else." It was one of the few times he didn't ask her to explain.

Her phone buzzed on the table like an angry hornet. She bounded away to text. It was probably Bryn, panicked over another stage set collapsing.

As he drove to work, anxiety pounded his insides. What was this job? What if Save Spring Valley wasn't supported by administration? When would *Tootsie* end?

It helped to count crosses and flower memorials for accident victims along the serpentine highway. There were thirteen, and that restored his calm. Regarding the job: Elsa was simply managing their finances. She also said a second job would mean better vacations, like his dream to fly on the Space Shuttle and sail to the Galapagos. More money would mean they could someday leave the rented split-level. By the time he parked in the faculty lot, he comprehended her second job.

Meanwhile, this virtual worlds project would be irresistible to a school anxious to overcome last year's abysmal test scores. And what if this led to a journal article, maybe even awards? It might mean money, which would make Elsa proud, and then they could take a trip. It had been almost two years, or 692 days, since their honeymoon in a little bed-and-breakfast, an old farmhouse in the middle of dying tobacco fields in North Carolina.

Andy headed at top speed to the computer lab, his blood buzzing from thoughts of Elsa in that bed. He almost collided with Mark, the former typing teacher with 142 days until retirement and resentful gatekeeper of the aging lab of machines.

"I have to schedule my virtual worlds project," Andy said. "I need ten days, seventh period, starting October 29th."

He watched Mark's lip arch, then descend in what Elsa said was the man's signature smirk. "We can't do that. *Second Life's* unsafe. There've been rapes and all kinds of shenanigans."

"It's not *Second Life*," Andy said. "It's a controlled environment sponsored by Jannus Technology Institute. There are limited pathways and predetermined avatars."

"Doesn't matter," Mark said, looking pleased for some reason Andy couldn't understand. "You know these kids. They can't be trusted. Look at that!" He pointed at a monitor, F SKOOL scrawled on it in permanent marker. "I just told administration we should block Google because all these delinquents do is abuse it."

"You can't ban the Internet," Andy said.

"Watch me. Parents don't want their kids on porn sites."

"But there are blocks and controls—" Andy began, but Mark had turned away. Andy wanted to throw something. It was with people like him that Andy desperately needed a translator. He wished Elsa were here.

Andy went straight to the principal, Brad. That was Elsa's advice whenever obstacles appeared in the form of colleagues: she said, "Call in the big guns." She also said it was important to schmooze administration. Andy wasn't sure what schmooze was, but he could safely assume it meant, Be polite.

After hearing Andy describe the project, Brad said, "Sounds great. Make sure you write a letter to the parents, set up rules for navigating the virtual space, and get some assistants. I'll talk to Mark."

Elsa could assist! She was free during her seventh, and it would only take her 5.5 minutes to get here from the high school campus.

Ball Number Three: click!

Later that day as Andy launched a PowerPoint lecture on asexual reproduction, Jimmy Jones called Franklin an asexual fag. The class laughed, Franklin turned red, and Andy told Jimmy to come with him into the hall.

"It's impossible to be asexual and homosexual," he told Jimmy.

"All y'all are fags!" Jimmy yelled. "I'll call y'all what I want, pussy motherfuckers!"

Andy flagged an assistant principal standing at the end of the hall.

Though Andy tried to catch Franklin after class, he bolted.

Andy texted Elsa after school but got no response. He really needed her to verify he had done the right thing, especially because she always said things could be so fragile with a kid like Franklin on the verge of a breakthrough. She always said "fag" equaled an automatic out—straight to the principal's office. Jimmy had been dealt with appropriately. But what about Franklin? How did one deal with him? What did you say after such insults, to a boy who hated conversation? No teacher had ever come after Andy when kids were terrifying, never tried to test his feelings, look for indicators, sample for the concentration of sadness inside his chest. Andy knew that even if they had, he could have only stared back at the interloping adult with wide eyes and frozen mouth.

Andy waited in his classroom for her text, counting octopi tentacles on his National Geographic poster, then bricks in the wall, then linoleum squares. His 122 books got shelved by height and descending order, and then color coded in gradations of deep hue to pastel. He scoured the classroom, picking up litter, and on the final tour, spotted one last piece of paper balled up beneath a desk in the back row.

He walked over and uncrinkled it. Written in faint pencil, lines radiating from it like a small sun, was the word SUICIDE. On the desk near it, fresh graffito in pencil: *Nature is a whore.*

He texted Elsa and waited another excruciating five minutes, his heart gunning like a desperate engine. Who wanted to die? Must solve this—must!

He ran through the seating chart for each class: first period, Brandon; second, Tammy Lynn; fourth, Jasmine; sixth, KD; and seventh, Franklin. Why would any student write "suicide" to look like a sun? He must talk to someone or his heart might overheat. Deanne! His teammate was the other person besides Elsa who could help him solve the puzzles of kids.

He found her in her classroom grading essays. "Hello, Deanne. How are you doing this afternoon? Do you have time for conversation?"

"Anything for you, honey." Deanne dropped her red pen and leaned forward on fat elbows.

"I don't know what this means. It looks like a student wrote it."

Deanne took the paper and smoothed it, her finger ragged with torn cuticles. "Light pencil and sun's rays," she said, her voice softening. "Says, *Look at me, but don't.*"

"What?"

"Just an old broad, jawing. What else you got, Mr. Spock?"

"It was near a desk where Brandon, Tammy Lynn, Jasmine, KD, and Franklin sit. On the desk was a new graffito: 'Nature is a whore.'"

"Good work." She gave him a smile that reminded him of Elsa's congratulatory taps on the nose. "Whoever it is—and I'm betting it's a he—he likes Nirvana." She pushed herself up with a groan and waddled to her file cabinet. She fumbled in a drawer and produced a cassette. She tapped lyrics on the inside of the front cover and held them up, nodding. "Yep. That boy in the green cardigan is still a menace."

Andy said, "Franklin loves Nirvana! Is this enough to assume it's Franklin?" The conclusion was unscientific, but he could hear Elsa scoff, saying science couldn't help you raise a kid.

"I don't know, honey, but *somebody's* depressed." Deanne peered at him, her watery blue eyes red at the rims. If Deanne were not already diabetic, she would be, soon. "The football players give him hell in my class."

"Yes, yes: Jimmy Jones."

"They probably think he's gay."

"Oh." Andy suddenly saw two unrelated bits of data connect: 1) Franklin leaning too close to Jimmy during lab work and Jimmy jumping back like he'd been stung; and 2) Franklin coming back from the bathroom with his face dripping and Jimmy falling out of his chair, laughing like a hyena. When Andy had asked Franklin why his face was wet, Franklin had said, "I had to wash all the smells off." That made perfect sense to Andy. These incidents plus today's incident equaled bullying, perhaps due to assumed homosexuality. The CNN report the other day had cited increased bullying as one potential cause in the rise of teen depression and suicide. Things were lining up in the Franklin column.

Deanne studied Andy. "What's your gut say? When you think of all the kids who come through your room, does Franklin go *ding ding ding*?"

Why she sounded like a bell he had no idea, but by "gut" he knew she meant intuition. Andy once asked Elsa whether intuition resided in the *cardia*, the *fundus,* the *corpus*, or the *pylorus*. To which Elsa said, "Either you get it or you don't," leaving him confused and irritated.

"It's a legitimate hypothesis," Andy said. "Franklin has few friends. Jimmy harasses him. Franklin is often angry. But that's different than sad."

"Yes and no." Deanne's look seemed sad, too, but Andy couldn't say why or for whom. "Seems like you know the kid. Ask if he left this note."

"But I don't know how."

"I see you talking to him after school all the time."

It was easy to listen to Franklin's high-speed chatter while Andy tended the snake, the iguana, and the hermit crabs. Franklin talked about Nirvana, OCD Clown, Green Day, and a band called Hüsker Dü—foreign to Andy, who followed Elsa's retro tastes of eighties and nineties pop. He said, "Can you write down what I should say?"

Deanne gave him a look of raised eyebrows he could not interpret. She wrote questions on the back of a hall pass. While she did, Andy counted 307 folders piled in one corner of her classroom, and noted a column of stapled papers in another, crowned with rosettes of dust bunnies. She handed him the pass and explained what he should say, depending on Franklin's answers.

Andy left with one piece of paper and at least two doubts. How was this a rational method of conducting an investigation? He felt a low level of distress, like the background hum of a machine about to fail. What if one false move by a teacher destroyed a kid's fragile ecosystem? Andy remembered every teacher's treatment of him since kindergarten, and he couldn't disagree with Elsa's raging that each had made "huge mistakes": placing him in the slow group, giving him repeated detentions for tapping and counting, and erupting with labels of "retarded" and "robot" in front of other students. Tears and panic attacks had been regular occurrences through the fifth grade. Though he had managed to stop crying by sixth grade, Andy could not remember whole sections of his middle-school experience. Perhaps he had wanted to die, too; maybe this was why the memories stayed black. What if he said or did something that made Franklin more agitated? What if Franklin went home and found a knife, or pills, or a gun?

At home, Andy gagged on any food he tried to eat, even the white bread. He sat on the floor in front of ESPN and clutched his knees, rocking back and forth until his breath grew regular.

Elsa did not come home at eleven. When Andy woke at 3:03 a.m., throbbing down below, he saw Elsa's body next to him, at least a foot away, curled in a tight ball. He put his hand on her shoulder. She shuddered in her sleep.

She was gone before he woke. Her note on the kitchen table said, "Lead on probation bcuz of drug possession. DAMMIT!!!! Ass hat walked on sets, have to repaint. This show is a nightmare."

Her excuses for being so late were rational, but still he felt panicky all during first period.

She texted him during second: *karaoke?*

Now everything was better. It had been more than a year since they had done karaoke, their tradition throughout college and years of living together before marriage. Andy felt a surge of what he secretly called happy-happy-joy-joy. She remembered! He didn't know why, but this outing, it meant everything was better, and everything would be okay.

He texted her, *gr8. must talk 2 suicidal kid*

who

Franklin?

right the gay one

don't know 4 sure

o come on

advice? come over and help plz

She didn't text back.

During lunch, Andy wrote a flow chart for speaking with Franklin, then asked Deanna to approve each of the optional paths for questions and answers. At the end of seventh, Andy asked Franklin to stay after. Franklin's eyes grew wide, his long lashes almost girlish. Andy said, "Don't worry, you're not in trouble."

After all the other kids had left, Andy shut the door on kids shoving and yelling in the hall. Deanne had said, "Make the conversation private." He crammed himself into a desk and beckoned Franklin to sit across from him.

Franklin sat. He stared at the desk. Today his shaved head looked gray with stubble.

Andy said, "I have to ask you a question." He showed Franklin the evidence. "Did you write this?"

Franklin looked at it, then looked at Andy. "Yeah."

Andy almost said, *That was easy.* Deanne had hypothesized

silence, denial, or tears. He looked at his script. "I'm concerned. Have you ever thought about hurting yourself?"

After a minute, Franklin said to the desk, "I think a lot worse than that."

"What do you mean?"

Franklin was silent so long, Andy worried the conversation was over. If Franklin had not thought about hurting himself, then liability was not an issue for the school. Andy said, "Suicide is definitively the worst option."

Franklin's face flushed hot pink. Tears brimmed on his lower lashes. "I *hate* my life!"

Andy looked around the room for Kleenex, a woman, anything. This was very hard to watch. In his memory, a tiny light flickered, swinging like a weak bulb above a scene with his mother when he was seven. Her yelling at him in the driveway for hugging the neighborhood boys. Andy never wanted sex with boys; they were for hugging and games. Girls were for kissing and more. But his mother didn't understand. She called him a queer and a freak.

Franklin rubbed his eyes like he might tear them off his face.

Andy said, "Is it because of what Jimmy did yesterday?"

Franklin shook his head.

Andy checked his paper. "Is there something happening with your family?"

"They don't understand."

"Don't understand what?"

Another pause. "Thoughts."

"Thoughts are just...thoughts," Andy said. "They can be managed." He wondered if he should share his counting formulas with Franklin, how primes helped so very much.

Now Franklin's head hung so low, Andy felt panic rise. Could this interview be considered a failure? Then he remembered Elsa saying one time, "Tell a story. That's how I connect. They need to leave every day with an Elsa story."

Andy said: "When I was growing up, I heard a lot from my mom about 'bad thoughts.' She said not to think certain things or you would go to hell. Well, I thought all of them, and I'm okay." Like wanting to hug other boys and wanting only the Five Food Groups. He figured this was a time to smile at Franklin, so he did, and saw Franklin was listening. This was a good time to share another nugget of Elsa wisdom. "Sometimes we feel things society says are bad, but they aren't."

Franklin's eyes widened.

If only Andy could know what the bad thought was. A worthy hypothesis was sex, though he could not read whether Franklin was heterosexual, homosexual, or bisexual. Andy said, "Some guys think too much about girls, and some guys think too much about guys. Hetero or homosexual, people become uncomfortable when encountering these facts."

Franklin stared at him like he was a train wreck. The spastic clock wheezed in the quiet.

Andy said, "You didn't answer my question. Have you thought about hurting yourself? There are people who can help."

Franklin's silence vibrated like a huge balloon straining at its sides. He said in a monotone, "Will you tell?"

At the sight of Franklin's flat dark eyes Andy felt a twinge deep in his stomach. "I have to. Do you have these thoughts?"

A muscle twitched in Franklin's cheek. "Yeah."

Andy said, "I need to tell the counselor. Let's go to the office."

Franklin sat still so long Andy's heart banged. What if he refused? Deanne had said, "If he admits it, don't let him out of your sight." She had also offered to speak to the counselor so she was ready for a potential visit.

Finally Franklin stood. They walked to the front office.

When the counselor, whose name Andy could never remember, looked up from her desk and saw Franklin's face, Andy saw something shift—a softening of the lines in her face. It was the look he had seen many mothers give their children, though never from his own.

"This boy has thoughts of su—" Andy began.

"I've got this," she said.

He patted Franklin on the back, but Franklin didn't look at him.

Andy drove straight to the high school. Elsa was not running practice on stage, and he could not find her in her trailer. It didn't help that twenty-seven hours had passed since any ball had clicked; the Franklin episode had stalled work on Spring Valley.

Wait—she had a job now. He called the Dollar Store. The clerk said this was not Elsa's day to work. What about rehearsals? She always said they were sacred, and the play was in trouble. It wasn't like Elsa to skip one.

The only way to fight his growing sense of dread was to count Ohio and Virginia license tags as he drove, and then get back to school as fast as he could to work on Spring Valley.

He pulled into the middle school, sweating, and rushed to Deanne's room.

She surveyed his face and said, "You look rattled. Did you take him to the office?"

"Yes."

"Better alive and hating you than..."

"Than what?"

"Honey, better than suicide!"

"Oh, right," Andy said. He had already forgotten about Franklin since the hand-off. "But this Spring Valley simulation will stimulate Franklin's interest. Can you be a T.A.?"

"Just a second, Spock; you're switching gears without a clutch. Do I have to know about fungus or lower intestines?"

"No, it involves disease epidemiology."

"Ugh—like that's better! I can't be a T.A., honey, but I'll help you supervise."

"You don't have to know facts. Elsa will be there, and she's a theater and English teacher."

Deanne snorted. "*There's* a house of cards."

"What?"

"Nothing."

Andy tried to read the lines on her face, suddenly taut. "What's wrong? Do you think it's unwise to do simulations with our limited computer resources?"

"I'll do it, I'll do it," Deanne snapped. She waved him off; he knew he'd been dismissed. It could be intuition telling him that Deanne meant something other than simulations. "A house of cards" was a metaphor. It helped to think of metaphors as equations. Something, the "house of cards"— call it x—was flimsy and subject to collapse. What was x?

Or it could also be random female behavior—crankiness, petulance—attributable to hormonal fluctuations.

For the first time in twenty-three days, Elsa came home early. 7:04 p.m. Andy met her at the door.

"I couldn't find you at school," he said. "I looked everywhere. You'll help me with this simulation, right?"

"Let me get inside first." Elsa edged around him, her arms laden with a box of empty beer bottles. She dumped the box on the kitchen counter and rubbed her eyes and sighed. Then she saw his face. "What are we panicking about now?"

"Deanne called the simulation or something related to it a 'house of cards'—as in unsustainable."

Elsa smirked. "That's because she's a Luddite."

"She's always got her kids in the lab."

"Yeah, typing essays," Elsa scoffed. "Big whup. No, this Franklin thing's got her spooked."

"I didn't observe that. She offered practical advice, and it worked."

Elsa sighed again and sat down at the kitchen table. Andy noted the dark circles under her eyes. "Andy, *she's* gay."

"She is?"

"More like non-practicing. They're everywhere in this closeted town." Elsa pulled four bottles by their necks from the box, opened the door between the kitchen and the garage, and dropped them in the recycling with a crash. More followed, like bombs.

Andy said, "What is upsetting you?"

Elsa shrugged and tossed in more. "Her sad, obese life—sneaking sips from a flask, kids' papers piling up like on *Hoarders*!"

Andy laughed because Elsa made Deanne sound like that reality TV show.

"Seriously!" Elsa grinned. "When she taught at the high school, she had *two years' worth of kids' papers* sitting in her classroom—untouched! She couldn't hack it at that level." Then she saw his face and amended, "I mean, the paper load—come on, you know what I mean!"

He walked into the den and turned on ESPN. So she thought teaching in a middle school was juvenile, if not unmanly. A little school, yielding a lesser salary.

She followed him in. "Baby, we're doing karaoke tonight, right? Come on now." She punched him in the arm.

"I said I'd go."

"Good. I'm making Bryn come. The little nerd needs to get out."

"I thought I was The Nerd," Andy said, but she'd already left the room.

That night, with enough beer in them to get their old college selves back (Elsa the Entertainer and Andy the Android), they laughed and joked as Elsa drove them to Bryn's. "God, she's such a neophyte," Elsa said. "I guess she thinks we can really bring bottles on stage during the party scene and have minors pretend to drink. So she hauls that big-ass box of bottles into practice, and the kids get all excited, and I'm like, 'Sweetheart, *no*."

Andy laughed. "Very stupid. This town would...put her in the stocks!"

"Exactly—full-on witch trial! I made the kids swear not to tell their parents."

That reminded him of this afternoon. He began to tell the story of Franklin. Elsa listened, asking questions about whether he was still following her advice to document unique student behaviors so he could learn to bond with students, and was he writing down next steps so he wouldn't forget, like following up with Franklin tomorrow. He was irritated when they pulled up to Bryn's place, a gray apartment complex on what Elsa called the white-trash side of town. "I know all this now," he said, "you don't have to teach me—"

"Bet they make Woo Woo here," Elsa said, leaning on the horn. She pointed at a dumpster.

"Woo Woo?"

Bryn dashed out a side door, her hair slicked back wet against her head. She looked like a 15-year-old boy.

"Bryn, how do they make Woo Woo?" Elsa demanded as she got in.

Bryn slammed the door, making the car shake. "Two parts cranberry grape juice, one part peach schnapps, one part vodka," she said, sniffing hard. Andy hoped she didn't have a cold. If she did, he would have to rinse out his nose several times.

"And where do you make it?" Elsa said.

"Water cooler or trash can."

"See?" Elsa said, nudging Andy, like he hadn't believed her.

"Astounding," Andy said.

Bryn snorted like all the phlegm in the world might be in her sinuses.

Elsa looked excited for some unknown reason and cranked the radio. "Ooh, yeah!" she shrieked, as "Tainted Love" blasted the car.

"Damn, you like old shit," Bryn said.

"But you wouldn't actually use a trash can, would you?" Andy said.

"Stop it with the 'old'!" Elsa cried. "Girl, I'm only twenty-nine!"

Karaoke was not like old times. Even though Elsa sang "Bette Davis Eyes" and Andy sang "She Blinded Me with Science," songs that used to make them laugh, Bryn's kittenish behavior about getting on stage absorbed Elsa most of the evening. Andy's role got switched to designated driver. He drank only half of Elsa's martini while the women drank themselves silly.

They dropped Bryn off at 1:00. At home, Elsa went right to sleep, her face flushed.

Andy woke at 3:00 again. Elsa curled like a pale little sow bug next to him, resisting touch. Now he saw comparisons everywhere and he did not like them.

He sat up. He'd been doing lab work in his dreams,

running a thought experiment over and over. Deanne did not mean a real house, like this split-level Elsa hated, saying it smelled of musty mountain. Deanne, who Elsa said was gay, once worked next door to Elsa at the high school. Next door, next door. What if Deanne had made a pass? At this time of the morning, this type of narrative speculation pulsed with logic.

Acid rose in his throat. He got out of bed. The room was dark save the GPS clock, accurate to the half-second, showing 3:47. He went downstairs to the computer.

Andy logged on to Facebook to see his wife's page. She had uploaded a new photo, replacing the picture of them chaperoning prom last spring. Now her sexy black-and-white head shot from senior year in college stared back at him: her dark hair, long and sleek, spilled down her chest; her nose lifted as if the entire world sat beneath her. Elsa as Lady Macbeth was stunning. Andy had come to every show, and every night she had pointed to him as the BFF in the front row. He proposed to her at the cast party. They had married five years later, to the day.

On Elsa's wall, Bryn, with a cartoon of a Berenstain Bears cub as her profile picture, had posted at midnight: CALLING U ON THE CARPET.

ELSA: why?

BRYN: TIRED OF YR LIP

ELSA: u want lip service?

BRYN: YES MAM

ELSA: :-)

What did "calling u on the carpet" mean? And why did Elsa insert a happy-face emoticon as her last response? There was a strange echo to the wall-to-wall posts, a pattern he had seen before. Like the IMs he and Elsa had exchanged in college when sitting across campus in single-sex dorms—

messages intimate with special knowledge. Perhaps Elsa and Bryn were growing too close with all these hours together. Elsa drew all kinds to her. But Elsa must realize if Deanne once had a crush, the boyish Bryn might be dazzled, too.

Andy knew he didn't understand a lot of things, but he did understand sex.

The next week was Spirit Week at both schools in honor of Homecoming. High school football would occupy the town a full five days. Andy's best plan for keeping restless kids on task would be the Spring Valley lesson, even with all its *x* factors. He congratulated himself for such excellent timing.

Deanne said Andy should keep a special watch on Jimmy Jones, who she said was full of "testosterone and warfare." Andy changed the seating chart in seventh so that Jimmy and Franklin sat at opposite ends. Franklin was quiet in class now. He no longer stayed after school with Andy. Andy noted these changes but had too much prep left for Spring Valley to think much more of it. Andy hoped the counselor had solved Franklin's problem. Surely there had to be a solution. If she explained logically that more and more people were accepting of homosexuality today, perhaps Franklin could see that his future looked brighter than it ever had. Not since the Greek and Roman days did historical records indicate such acceptance of alternative lifestyles; surely Franklin could see his luck in being born now, not in some other era.

The morning of Retro Day, Elsa came down to the kitchen dressed as if she lived in the eighties: a big boxy black jacket, a skinny red satin tie, skinny black jeans, and an oversized red bow in her hair. She mocked Andy for refusing to wear a costume. Andy told her not only was it distracting but he didn't understand attachments to historical eras. He reminded her about the Spring Valley kickoff.

"What time again?" she said, poking a lone dangling earring through a lobe.

Andy said with an edge, "Your free period." Several administrators would be visiting; how could she forget? He had described to her countless times all the pitfalls. "You have to be there," he said, voice rising and lungs tightening. "What if kids wander around the Valley texting cuss words? What if they fly their avatars too fast, like jet fighters, and the guests think everything's out of control? I really need you there on time!"

"Chillax, dude," she said, tossing a dish towel at him. The corner cuffed him in the cheek, almost nicking his eye.

"I'm not your dude," he said. "You need to stop acting like a kid on Facebook."

For a nanosecond, her eyes glazed over like a system crash, and her mouth went slack. Then she snapped back: "Why are you stalking my page?"

"What if Bryn has a crush on you, like Deanne?" He heard his voice rise. The desire to count every diamond in the linoleum surged through him.

"Don't mention that sow. Goddammit, I don't have time for this!" Elsa stomped over to the sink and crashed dishes under hot water. "You think everyone's obsessed with sex— me, Franklin, Bryn, but you've got the problem!"

She stormed out the back door. He heard her scooter growl to life and putter away.

When she was like shrapnel exploding in his face, it had to be her period. This morning, her status update was HATE BEING ON THE RAG. Seven comments followed from commiserating females, including students. But this conclusion did not satisfy. What if his hypothesis about Bryn—thin in many respects—drove Elsa away? Like the clinging hugs he once gave other boys?

He could not lose her.

During seventh period, five administrators took their places at the back of Andy's classroom. Brad had told district officials this simulation could be a model curriculum for all middle schools, which was why he invited an assistant principal, the superintendent, the assistant superintendent for curriculum and instruction, and the director of academically gifted programs.

As the bell rang, Franklin came in wearing a t-shirt with pink and yellow teddy bears. The class exploded with laughter. Administrators exchanged glances. "Fag in drag," Jimmy said, to the great delight of those near him.

"Listen please!" Andy shouted. "Who remembers what we're doing today?"

"Something lame," Jimmy yelled. "How come we can't have a Wii?"

It took them five minutes to follow Andy's directions about finding pens and notebooks and settling down.

Andy had them walk to the lab in something resembling a line, administrators trailing, all looking grim and whispering.

Inside the lab, Deanne and Mark waited. Deanne said with a smirk, "Where's your other half?"

Mark said, "Don't use computers five, seven, and twenty-two. I can't figure out what's wrong with them."

Andy told everyone to sit down at a station and log on. Where was Elsa? Deanne grabbed his wrist. "Focus, Andy," she said under her breath.

Jimmy shoved Franklin off station four, but Deanne made him get up and go to another row so Franklin could stay. She and Mark circulated, pulling kids off Facebook, Twitter, and celebrity gossip sites, while Andy shouted instructions. "Remember what's appropriate avatar behavior! Teams, stay in contact using the text box! Don't forget to check water runoff to low-lying areas! Remember some houses have septic! And visit overcrowded parts of the city!"

Deanne made the rounds, a slow and grandmotherly tugboat pulling distracted kids back into the simulation. She settled those screeching for help. Soon the room buzzed with concentration. Everyone forgot about Franklin's t-shirt.

After several minutes of silent screen study, Franklin's hand shot up. Andy came over. Franklin said, "My hypothesis is it could be insects and septic runoff into the river."

"Very good. Cite your evidence of potential sources of contagion in your journal," Andy said.

Franklin looked lit from within. It was the first time Andy had ever seen Franklin concentrate on anything other than music or hair.

The administrators strolled through rows, peering over student shoulders at screens, murmuring with solemn nods: a good sign. Even Mark lost his sour look as kids stayed on task.

Elsa never showed.

When the bell rang, Brad gave Andy a thumbs-up. The superintendent stalked over on three-inch heels, careful to avoid brushing against desks and chairs. She shook Andy's hand and simpered, "Very brave experiment, Mr. Swindon. Kudos to you. Though I have to say, what a strange future if this is where curriculum is headed. I hope we never lose face-to-face class. Otherwise it's children leading hard-wired virtual lives."

The assistant superintendent for curriculum and instruction, a puny man, followed close behind, nodding like a bobblehead doll. The superintendent added, "Well, at least they're solving real problems in their fake world." Her entourage chuckled as she dusted off her Chanel purse and clacked out. Her calves looked like firm cuts of taut, ripe muscle. Elsa had never in her life worn a pair of heels. Why, right at this moment, that struck Andy as a huge loss, he had no idea.

Deanne squeezed his shoulder, startling him. "Congrats, honey. You're a champ." Her look was full of something more complex than sadness.

Driving home, Andy tapped the dashboard 149 times. He made seventy-three perfect circles on the steering wheel. Who cared if he won the attention of district officials? It didn't mean anything if his wife didn't show for his most important class ever.

At home on the kitchen counter sat a note from Elsa:

Andy. I'm sorry. It's been a shitty week. Will make it up to you. With Bryn tonight. It's just a thing.

I'm here for YOU, always. Don't forget that.

You're free too. Life will be so much better if we're both 100% fulfilled.

Society is judgmental but this can work.

He went to their bedroom. Her side of the closet was full. Only an overnight bag was gone.

Andy sat up that night drinking a case of beer and watching the World Series. He thought about calling Ray, divorced twice, who partnered with another guy against him and Elsa in fantasy baseball. Ray sometimes e-mailed or called with stats he found intriguing. Maybe Ray would come over and watch the game. But it was better to sit at home texting or calling rather than wasting time driving. You could have the same experience staying home.

Maybe the superintendent was right. His lesson was fake epidemiology, not face-to-face reality. No, she was wrong; the lesson was a success. Andy drew a flow chart onto the coffee table with his Sharpie. He must know how things happened. In the beginning, there was the brilliant idea, brought to him by Franklin and Crunchettos. Draw an arrow to Google, which led to Jannus Technology. Then Brad, Deanne, Mark—why, his colleagues had been more help than Elsa! How could that be?

By the fifth inning and the sixth beer, Andy had invented seventeen avatars for a problem-based learning scenario. Andy Valley—a stroke of genius! A place where solutions for multicausal problems were imminent, where broken kids like Franklin saved the world! Andy's version also starred a pandemic, where the virus would be fatal to certain populations and would be allowed to mutate. Meanwhile, he would plague the region with political instability. Imagining details was child's play; the challenge would be building the virtual space. That would take many weeks and serious money. There would also be the challenge of supervising students in a world with many avatars and portals sending them down separate paths. How to create a locked-down, disease-ridden Shanghai, Islamabad, or New Orleans—but with virtual chaperones? He would be the one to do it!

He was now quite drunk and laughed out loud at his swarming ideas. Armed with swords and lasers, kids could ward off disease, wreaking razor-sharp vengeance against microbes and illogical outcomes. He could do more than line up avatars like chess pieces. He could infuse them with at least seven emotions and complicate emotional interrelations. He would connect their squares, their dots, their stories.

Franklin needed to hear this new scheme. No doubt right now he was trolling Facebook. Test-drive the idea, beta-test with the tastemakers, with the youth, the eternally youthful—

Andy raced to his Mac. It sang to him a loyal, familiar tune.

THE FLAT AND WEIGHTLESS
TANG-FILLED FUTURE

R ONALDA LIGHTS A CAMEL BUT leaves it burning on an egg-crusted plate. Everywhere she sees what needs doing: stovetop glazed with grease, counters studded with crumbs, corners laced with cobwebs. She swabs the counter while the boys' jeans clink against dryer walls, while the baby squalls from the living room, while her head spins as fast as that silly, don't-go-breakin'-my-heart song jabbering on the radio. Thank goodness Diane's coming through the door, no knock needed.

Diane glides in, all legs in shiny red running shorts, shorter than are decent, but at least she only wears them here, what she calls her "second home."

Diane points at the cup on the counter. "Let me guess. Cup's full, but the coffee's cold?"

Ronalda starts to say, "Fill her up again," the cue for Diane to make a fresh pot while Ronalda changes the baby. Instead Ronalda says, "This cup's half-empty and I'm half-dead."

"I'll fix us some fresh and we'll have us a good sit-down." Diane pours coffee down the sink and rinses the cup.

"Sit-down? When?" Ronalda says. "I want you to look. This filth—and all the beds unmade."

The baby's wailing so hard he's choking. She heads to

the tiny living room where the sun is already strong like a fist behind the shutters. Maybe one day it will melt the whole world and send a flood of tar, creosote, and pop-tops pouring through these windows. Even then they still won't have the money to paint or furnish this room that could make a home civilized. Things get dark at the edges as she leans over the playpen and lifts Bradford, red-faced and snot-nosed, heavy as a stone. "Stop it," she snaps. "This ain't the day. *This ain't the day.*" Funny how Diane just passed him by, the boy screaming like a banshee. Then again, Diane's done her time with her own three.

Ronalda carries Bradford to the kitchen, jouncing and shushing. She grabs a dishrag sitting in the sink and wipes his face. Crying turns to hiccups.

"I think you're a poet," Diane says. The percolator behind her goes *glub, glub, glub.*

Ronalda laughs. "Law, me who never graduated?" She grabs a diaper from the stack on the kitchen table.

"'This cup's half-empty and I'm half-dead.' It's got a rhythm to it." *Glub, glub, glub.*

Ronalda shakes her head. What kind of hog path is Diane running down now?

Diane says, "You're smart, emotions kind of smart."

"Crazy's more like it."

"Remember how you said boys only bring trouble and traction while girls bring the high drama and heartache? Where'd you get that from?"

"I don't know, I just get stupid sometimes."

"How about the time you said we got to have flowers to look at so our hearts can grow back every morning?"

"You know my zinnias are doing great. Only this one, *he* don't smell like a flower." She taps Bradford's bulky bottom and he giggles. Diane doesn't care a lick about flowers and jokes that she's got a black thumb, so Ronalda has given up hinting about the Strayers' dandelion yard, sorrier than keeyarn.

Diane says, "I'm going to make me a book of Ronnie sayings."

"Make me that cup while I get him changed. Law! It is hotter than a match in here."

Ronalda leaves with Bradford for the bathroom. She lays him on a towel on the counter and unpins him. The old diaper hits the floor. Sweat drips from her nose. She swabs his bottom with wet tissue. She wraps him with the fresh cloth and seals the deal with duck-shaped pins she used on the other two. She sits him on the bath mat while she shakes the turds from the old diaper into the toilet and flushes. Bradford squeals when she dips the diaper in the fresh water and wrings it out. The diaper hits the pail with a wet clang. As she scrubs off in the sink, she sees her hands aging faster than the rest of her, red and lined and ragged with hangnails. No poetry in these paws.

When Ronalda comes back with Bradford, Diane has the radio turned up to "If You Leave Me Now," mournful and begging. "Ronnie, songs are like poetry, you know? What I meant to say was, you got what they call 'a turn of phrase.'"

New coffee gives a dying gurgle. The smell is all of a sudden turning her stomach. Not a good sign. Ronalda says, sharper than she means, "I don't know about no turning phrases. You're the one turning heads."

Diane looks startled. Then she says, "Bobby don't—he doesn't seem to look anymore."

"Then he ain't got sense to get out of the rain. Look at you—hair not a bit gray and legs a mile long; you would look good on the TV." Ronalda does not add, Bobby's always been a fool. "You got a case of think-too-much."

Diane says, soft, "*O teach me how I should forget to think.*"

"What's that?" Ronalda sits Bradford in the high chair and rifles through the cupboard.

"Something I read." Diane gets pink, grabs cups from the shelf, then looks hopeful. "You ever read Shakespeare?"

Ronalda pulls out a jar of applesauce. "They made us back in school, but I never could keep my eyes on it. Mama always said, 'Books collect the dust.' Traded all of ours except the Bible one time at the swap meet."

"I been picking it up again—*Romeo and Juliet*? Kind of sounds like the Bible."

Ronalda wonders whether that's blasphemous. Instead she says, "Darryl took me to that movie one time, that Zepparella one. All I remember was it had naked bodies in it. Darryl took it so serious. I was teasing him and I said, 'Look at you, all tore up'—but he just kept saying, 'It ain't right. No way out. Fate's got us all screwed.' I couldn't make heads or tails of it."

"He must have meant the Prince," Diane says. "He's the one who said, 'All are *punnashed*.'" She looks dreamy, like she might take off with those long legs, shoot into the sky like a Hollywood starlet, an Esther Williams riding fountains.

"Funny how they talk," Ronalda says. "How do you keep it straight? And who has the time?" She wrestles with the lid.

"Here, give it," Diane says. She taps the jar against the counter, then uses a dishrag. The jar pops and she hands it back. "What I wouldn't give for some time. But I can't help thinking."

Ronalda finds a bowl and a baby spoon. Bradford waves his arms. The sauce is slow coming but finally glops into the bowl. She puts some in his mouth.

Diane says, "Don't you ever want to, you know, figure it all out?"

Ronalda feels her too-close stare. "What's to figure?" Suddenly her heart starts hammering; she doesn't know why. "Mama used to say, the more you stir the s-h-i-t, the more it stinks. That enough poetry for you?"

Diane cackles. "Yes'm. I don't know, I just like imagining things. How life's like a bunch of doors—you know, like *The Price is Right:* Door Number One or Door Number Two? Which you going to choose?"

Ronalda points at Bradford. "One of these and you got no choice." He waves fat fists at them, beaming, his face muddy with applesauce. They laugh and he gurgles, deep and chugging like an old man with phlegm.

Diane taps red nails on the counter. "Ye-e-es, babies do slam the door on some things." Ronalda sees the shadow cross Diane's brow quick as a summer storm. Diane catches her looking and puts on her happy face.

Ronalda says, nice as she can, "Don't be like Darryl, driving himself crazy asking what if this and that. I tell him, 'Shut off the brain, it's closing time.'"

Bradford screeches as Diane says, "Well, it's just so hard."

"What's that?"

"It don't matter." Then Diane says, "Well, that's new. Isn't that nice." She points at the family portraits Ronalda had taken at JCPenney and finally got hung late last night: Laird with his new college girlfriend, that skinny thing who needs a good mama; Ronalda with Darryl and the three boys, her grin too crooked but her eyes about closed from the bliss of getting them all in the same room; and her and Bradford, drool glistening on his chin, but at least not colicky. What doesn't fit is Kenny, always the sullen monkey-in-the-middle, fifteen and furious: he flat refused to smile in any of them. It still eats at her.

"We come a long way from that," Diane says, pointing at the tinted one, moved to a lower tier beneath the new glossies. In another age, back in Saxapahaw, long before life in Charlotte, Ronalda grins in a dress made from a flour sack, tiny blue flowers she used to think pretty. Darryl stands next to her, gangly with a flat-top and a face full of acne, proud as punch to be with his girl on the stoop of the old homeplace.

"Yes I have." Ronalda's head gets light again, then taut at the temples. That photo goes back twenty years but feels like someone took it this morning, like someone shoved her on a spaceship and sent her right into the flat and weightless Tang-filled future.

"Where's one of you and me?" Diane says.

"We need to get one done, don't we."

"I know what. I'm going to snap one of you scrubbing the floor. That's you all over."

Me scrubbing and you watching, Ronalda thinks. But all she says is, "I tell you, it never gets done. Every day you get up and there it is to do all over again."

Bradford smacks her on the arm. Ronalda pours more sauce in the bowl.

Diane says with a grin, "I think you like all the cleaning and keeping busy. You never come over and just *sit.*"

What to say? Diane's place is so, well, dirty. Though Diane always looks like a picture; Ronalda can't abide those who can't keep neat.

Diane keeps on about her new Polaroid camera and how much she loves it while Ronalda feels her eyes glaze over, fuzzy with a new kind of tired she hasn't felt since—*law, don't even think.*

The dryer buzzes and Diane jumps. "Loud as the apocalypse!" Diane says. "Lord, I will never get used to that. Anyway, meant to tell you, Flannery called."

"Don't say." Flannery is the one who left and has boys by two different men. How she came from good people, Ronalda doesn't know. Well, yes she does: Bobby used to be no good. As for Diane's twins, Eudora and Katie Anne, there's hope yet. Least they can go to the bathroom by themselves, and Diane can leave them for a spell while they play in the sprinkler.

Bradford plunges his hand in the bowl and flings sauce on the floor; Ronalda grabs the dishrag and mops him off, then the floor, then tosses the dishrag back in the sink.

"Got herself a job," Diane is saying.

"Good for her." Ronalda's knees creak as she straightens from the squat.

"How'd you get Laird to go to college?"

"Don't know. He just wanted it." Suddenly Ronalda's throat fills up with throbbing nausea; she has to swallow hard against it.

"How'd you get him to *want* it?"

"Couldn't tell you." Ronalda steadies herself against the counter and swallows again. "Least he helps us pay." She yanks the cupboard door open, finds the Saltines, and scrambles in the box. She stuffs three in her mouth.

"Flannery don't seem to be the type to go, ever."

Because she's a spitting image of Bobby, Ronalda thinks. Meanwhile, Laird is just like Darryl. If Flannery had one ounce of Diane's or Darryl's kind of brain, then maybe...

"If I'd gone to Carolina..." Diane is saying, looking dreamy. "Well, I wouldn't have got much done. I'd have followed Todd around like some pitiful thing. Son of a—" She gives Ronalda a devilish look.

"Don't say it." Ronalda focuses on crackers melting on her tongue. Bradford smacks his high-chair tray with sticky hands.

"Well, it's true. Didn't think he was the type to run....but he did get that scholarship. Can you blame him?"

A moment of silence for men who disappear when they fear girls are pregnant. Ronalda remembers the story different; the scholarship is a new twist. She can picture Diane still a girl in Elizabeth City, living for steamy nights beneath the bleachers and promises of honeymoons in Morehead City. She was left high and dry in those stands by one who could throw touchdown passes and smile like Paul Newman. Diane's daddy wasn't a farmer; he was a factory man. The girl had bought dresses all the time. Bought dresses that led to a big old scare. Ronalda does the math, wondering if she and Diane could have been friends if they'd lived in the same town; maybe not, since by that time Ronalda had dropped out and married Darryl, with Laird on the way. A silly door to go through, dwelling on things past and what-ifs.

Diane shakes her head. "Todd was sure handsome, but mean as a snake. He wouldn't have been any better."

Ronalda looks sharply at her. Husbands aren't brands to pull off a shelf. They are what you get, maybe even what you deserve. But all she says is, "Where's Flannery at?"

Diane says, "The Circle K," and her face twists with sadness. Finally: "It's a job."

"Yes, it is. It's like I keep telling Kenny, there's no shame in honest work."

"You and Darryl teach him right." Diane casts her eyes down at those long miles of leg. "Can't get it out of mind, my baby girl working a gas station. Always too busy to give me a call till it's too late."

Ronalda knows what kind of late she means, the-baby's-on-the-way kind of late. "Kenny hung on me when he was a baby. Now he don't have two words for me."

"Baaa!" yells Bradford. "Ba! Ba!"

"Says he'll run away and go live with Laird. Acts like he hates us, especially his daddy." Suddenly Ronalda wishes she could hit something; the boy can be that stupid. "Darryl made him quit that Record Bar. Has him running errands at the body shop."

"That Record Bar has too many delinquents."

"It's got too many colored. Owner's from up north. Got his hair this high"—Ronalda lifts her hand several inches above her head—"then scalped like an Indian on the sides. It's not right." She feels her heart speed up. "Did I tell you how Kenny's been sneaking out the last weekends, probably drinking and carrying on?"

Bradford screams. Ronalda shoves a big spoonful in. Diane squeals, "You like dat, little boy? That's right, you eat up." She comes over and rubs his bald head.

Bradford chokes and spits up. Diane backs off while Ronalda mops him off, sighing.

"Diane. You can pour me that coffee now." How can a woman fail to get the littlest thing done? Cold all over again.

Diane finds the cups again and pours. "Sit down. Your cigarette's half gone."

"I can't sit."

"You will when you fall down."

The radio shrills with horrible sound. Then the man says, "This is a test. For the next sixty seconds, this station will conduct a test of the Emergency Broadcast System. This is only a test." Another blast of sound. Bradford yelps and swats his ears.

With Diane's back turned, with the drowning blare, Ronalda hears herself blurt, "Darryl's cheating."

The signal cuts out and the man says, "This is a test of the Emergency Broadcast System. The broadcasters of your area in voluntary cooperation with the FCC..."

Diane has been holding the full cups forever, frozen like an ad for a cute waitress who'll serve you right. Bradford opens his mouth wide as a church door, waiting. Diane says, "How do you know? Have you seen her?"

"No."

"But how do you know?"

Not a question Ronalda expected. Bradford tunes up, eyes full of tears.

Diane keeps on. "Does he—ignore you?"

Ronalda's heart quivers like a bow scurrying across strings. "No more than usual." She's hit Diane with too much: dirty laundry of the worst kind. Ronalda waits for Diane to say the right words. She always says, *Darryl's a good, good man.*

Bradford starts to cry.

Ronalda scoops him up. Diane sets the cup at the end of the counter where Ronalda stands, jouncing Bradford. Usually Diane brings the sugar bowl and a spoon. Ronalda knows she's said it all wrong. She tosses Bradford even harder, walking around the kitchen table, then into the den to lower the radio that got her into trouble, then around the coffee table. Back into the kitchen, settling him on her hip, feeling her shoulder tweak, saying, "Come on now. Enough of that." He simmers down. She feeds him again, thinking maybe if she tells Diane about all the things she counted— how Darryl jerks in his sleep, hot with Jolene nightmares; what he said to her after the fireworks the other night; how he's got his head always somewhere else—then Diane would see.

"You say you feel half-dead." Diane sounds distant. Ronalda looks up, sees Diane's blank eyes, and panics: is Bobby cheating, too? Then they're all going to Hades tomorrow, this whole street.

Ronalda says to Bradford, and her eyes fill up: "Diane, it's killing me."

Diane picks at something stuck to the counter. "Men get thoughts. Long as they don't act, no harm in that. Am I right?"

Ronalda feels a lump in her throat so hard she can barely talk. "He stays in his room for hours. Plays George Jones all the time."

"That's it?" Diane looks relieved on top of curious.

"I've known the man since 1953. I know when his heart is somewhere else." Her heart pounds in her ears and a sweaty surge of anger comes over her, prickling everywhere. Maybe it's being thirty-eight with a one-year-old and two boys almost grown. Maybe it's being married to a man who kills himself at work every day. Maybe it's all just her body, the change come too early, or a period not come at all, making her crazy as a loon. But she thought Diane would at least ask about this woman, about how Ronalda imagines her, fills her out like a mannequin who blinks long lashes and twirls on stick legs. How every magazine at the grocery store shouts her many names along with the starlets' faces—could be Barbi, Patty, Farrah, Jaclyn. Diane should say not to worry, how this other woman is sorry and no-count, and even if Darryl has gone through that door, he's like to come back.

Diane watches the linoleum. Ronalda sees the grit there. The nail in the coffin, she wants to yell it—"He's taken up reading!"—but she doesn't, because so has Diane.

The front door bangs. Kenny bolts through the kitchen, a blur of curly blond hair too far past his ears and a tight t-shirt soaked with sweat. He sees them, grunts, "Hey, Mrs. Strayer," and heads for the room he used to share with Laird.

"What're you doing home?" Ronalda yells. "Not even noon!"

He hesitates, always with that cornered look about him, big pale eyes staring like a calf at a new gate. He says, "I quit."

"You what? Your daddy let you? How'd you get here?"

"I walked." Now he looks defiant.

"You walked?" Diane says. "Ronnie, that's five miles and some highway. Poor thing, look at him."

"Poor is right. Always wants the best of everything, now how's he going to get it?" Before Ronalda can catch a breath, Kenny disappears down the hall and into his room. In seconds the walls are shaking, beating with something about brats and baseball bats.

Diane laughs. "What is it—that's not even rock music!"

"I'm telling you, that's how he spends his money. That and her." Ronalda stuffs Bradford in the high chair. He screams.

"I got him." Diane moves at Bradford with a huge grin. "Gonna getcha!" She pokes a finger in his belly button and he giggles.

Ronalda hustles to the boys' room. The hallway is dark, and she stumbles on rippled carpet. Diane calls after, "Ask him who it is. I never heard such a racket, but now I'm curious."

"Kenyon Ray!" Ronalda bursts through his door.

"Mom, dang it!" Kenny is hunched over, stepping out of his jeans. He clutches them to his waist, glaring at her. From diapers to Fruit of the Loom in a heartbeat. The room buzzes and rattles with drums and electric guitar, beating so fast they could knock out walls.

"Turn that off! Your daddy's going to wring your neck!"

"He ain't here! When's he ever here!"

"You watch your mouth!" Her throat feels raw. There's been a lot of yelling lately.

"I'm changing! You ruin all my jeans!" He turns away from her, tossing them on the floor and reaching for another pair.

"What you mean, ruin? I don't see you doing laundry!"

"I keep telling you, don't put them in the dryer! They're all damn highwaters now. We can't afford anymore—that's what *you* always say."

Back still turned, he steps into a fresh pair, pale blue, tight against his bottom, so many years beyond a baby's.

"If you quit your job, then you got chores here. All day!" The room is a disaster with clothes, books, albums everywhere; on his bed, a black record cover with a ghostly silver triangle smack in the middle. It looks from the devil. That triangle might just be the long and the short of everything that's wrong. She stalks out, almost slamming the door.

The music lowers a few decibels, but the beat thunders on. Diane coos at Bradford, all smiles now, waving his arms.

"Went and quit a good job," Ronalda fumes. "Darryl will kill him. Diane, this might be it."

"He'll get another. He'll see when he can't buy records."

"He even told us he'd vote for Carter if he could."

"Lordy, lordy." Diane seems amused.

Ronalda's cigarette is ash, and something about the way Diane hovers over Bradford Ronalda just can't bear. She scoops him up. Bradford whimpers as she holds him tight.

Diane says, "Honey, it'll be all right."

What does Diane know? She's stopped wearing red lipstick, only pale pinks and oranges now, and she's stopped ratting her hair, just does curlers and spray. She even jokes about getting a pageboy. It's boy stuff, like girls getting into the Navy and bra burners in the streets, standing things on their head. It's not country but city, so far from places like where they came from, this city still not home. It's not family.

Ronalda blurts, "You don't know it'll be all right."

The music cuts off like someone pulled a plug. Kenny slouches out of his room, shirt fresh and hair combed. Waves of Brut aftershave surge everywhere as he comes up to the counter, picks up the phone, and dials.

"Who you calling?" Ronalda says.

He says into the phone, low, "Come get me? Bye."

"Where you going?"

"Karen's."

"How you getting there?" Ronalda already hates the answer.

"She's picking me up."

Ronalda considers whether to make him stay, but she doesn't want a fight in front of Diane. "This is between you and your daddy. Wait till he gets home. You'll see."

Kenny gives her a look that could break glass. Then he says politely to Diane, "Goodbye, Mrs. Strayer."

"Kenny, what's that music you're playing?" Diane says.

Kenny looks shy. "The Ramones."

"Where they from? I never heard a thing like it."

Kenny looks proud. "I think New York? It's so new they don't got a name for it."

Ronalda snaps, "Sounds like cats squalling."

Kenny's face reddens and he leaves the kitchen. Ronalda follows him down the hall and out the front door onto the stoop. "I don't like her collecting you," she says to his back.

Kenny turns and glares. "She doesn't *collect* me."

The sun is fierce out here, the air thick, and she can see a fine line of sweat dampening his fresh t-shirt, like someone ran a finger down his taut back. "She'll think she wears the pants."

"Give me a car and then we all get what we want." His eyes are so blank with casual betrayal, she gets dizzy. They all hate her. He starts down the steps.

"I'm taking away those records," she says. "No job, no nothing."

He stops. "Why don't you take all of Dad's," he says over his shoulder, and then under his breath, "Hypocrite."

"What'd you say?"

"Nothing. Least I'm honest."

"You don't make any sense." She hears her voice, faint against the sound of her heart beating crazy. What if she's got something wrong with her?

Kenny squints at the sky, then back at her, his look almost sedated. "I'm sick of all the lies."

"Tell me one lie I ever told you."

"It ain't you. Never mind. You don't get it."

"I get you're acting crazy. Don't get above your raising."

Tires squeal from a distance. Karen's butterscotch Mustang convertible pulls up.

"Spoiled rotten," Ronalda snaps. "I don't know how they afford it." She hears the phone ring back in the house. It's got to be Darryl, probably in a rage.

Kenny tumbles down the remaining steps, eager as a puppy for this blonde, her hair in bangs, the rest soft cascades falling away from her face. She smiles shyly and wiggles her fingers at Ronalda, other hand on the shift.

Kenny turns at the bottom and says, as if to a child, "This thing's fuel efficient."

Ronalda knows that's a cut against his daddy and his Bonneville, but the boy doesn't know a thing about cars; why, Darryl's new Trans Am...The phone keeps ringing. Kenny gets in the girl's car. Karen glances at Ronalda, almost apologetic, but then looks ahead as if something important is through that windshield.

They are gone. The thick air makes droplets crawl along her scalp and pool between sagging breasts. That new Trans Am. It's too silver and too clean. And tiny! You can't haul a gallon of milk in it. She hears the murmur of Diane answering the phone, saying, "It'll be all right. It's the age. They rebel. Don't do that. No. No. Give it a while. Give him time." Diane's voice is soft, firm, knowing. "I know. It's all right." Ronalda waits, chest tight, waiting for Diane to call, "Ronnie?" But she doesn't.

Then Diane says with words where you can hear the smile, "You, too." Soft. Then softer, "Take care." Words of a smart woman who knows what to say when teenagers stray. Who isn't about to faint or scream on this stoop. Words that can be said smooth as liquor to another woman's husband.

No. Not her. He might, just like a man, but not her. Him last week, July 4th. His whistling good mood as he hovered around Diane at the neighborhood picnic. Their jokes about barbecue and the swine flu, going on and on about wanting to see *All the President's Men,* talk that bored Ronalda to tears. Little things she sees now, like this chatter, like his talk with the receptionist at the body shop, and his smiles at the Sunday school leader at church, these words and the women suddenly painted loud in stripes of red, white, and blue.

No, Jesus, no. In the yard next door, Diane's twins skip through the sprinkler, a rotating spray with barely any pressure, giggling. Water looks like the River Jordan right now. What if she ran through just a second? Darryl would say she was a damn show.

"Hey, Mrs. Block!" calls Katie Anne.

Eudora says, "Whatcha doing?"

"Going crazy," Ronalda wants to say, but instead, "Hey girls, how you?"

"Come on over, Mrs. Block! We couldn't get Mama to! Please!"

Well, that's not right. You pay attention to your children. Ronalda feels her body moving down the steps, grass tickling her ankles, sweat pouring from every nook and cranny.

"Yay, she's coming! Tag, you're it!"

A small hand stinging her arm but that's okay, the water's light on her skin, more like a warm trickle, spattering her stiff hair and taut neck and jiggling torso. She chases the girls around and around through dandelions till the crabgrass spins and the brown patches look to come up in her face.

"Hahahahahaha!" Eudora shrieks, pointing at Ronalda's blouse –the white gone dark, stuck to her bra. Now the neighborhood can see her intimates.

Ronalda yells, "Learn some respect!" She steps on the hose. The sprinkler tilts and shoots into the bushes.

The girls' faces fall. Ronalda stalks around the corner of the house and twists the water off. "Get! I'm sending your mama over with a belt!"

The girls scatter.

Ronalda hustles from the yard, hands slammed across her breasts, feeling wild, not right. She bursts through the open door into the foyer and sees Diane like a light at the end of the hallway's dark channel, singing and waltzing Bradford around the yellow kitchen to "Afternoon Delight." He giggles. The curve of her arm as she twirls, the flash of a red manicure; the woman moves with angelic grace, like songs were made for her. Like she could slip right into the passenger side of a silver chariot with music swelling Zepparella style.

Now Ronalda knows what she knows. It's true, even if

she didn't find it in a book. She laughs, a cold hard bark, grim as a reaper come for his due.

She heads to their bedroom – the room that might have been a dining room but he said, "What use we got for that?" and built a door instead. It gave them and the boys their own rooms, but like all things in this house, he is the boss man, and she cleans up after. She squats before the stereo cabinet, pries it open, and yanks out all his LPs. Osborne Brothers, Jimmy Martin, Bill Monroe, Stanley Brothers, Buck Owens, the records slide across the carpet like a huge deck of cards. What if she broke the George Jones, ripped his smirking face off the cover? Her blouse feels slimy now, like another thick skin.

"Ronnie?" Diane calls from the kitchen, her voice light and breezy. Ronnie, not my name, don't call me that, even if the other fits like a shoe too tight. "You got a boy's name," said Will Hunt, the first day of first grade. "That name's ugly," said Betty King, whose daddy owned the supermarket, destroying all hopes of free Bit-O-Honeys. Ronalda went home that day and asked, "Why I got this name?"

"It's your daddy's," said her mother, not mean, but not nice either, just busy.

Ronnie seems fake as the AstroTurf that makes Darryl so mad, or credit cards, or gas prices. Never mind Diane's name isn't real; she once told Ronalda she picked it up when she moved here. Back home she was Harriet.

Ronalda sits down hard. Beneath her bottom, an LP cracks. She feels tears. What he said fourth of July, now it means the world: "Don't you ever stop long enough to think?"

Well, she did. And look what's happened now.

Once there were two, supposed to be one; now there are three. Well, then. Where there was one, make it two. Split the beds apart. He may be doing the adding, but she'll do the subtracting.

She moves to the beds, twins shoved together, since there's never enough to afford a queen but somehow, a damn new car. She squats and yanks one her way, budging it a few inches to this corner, now wrestling with the other, till there's a small channel between the two. Make it a canyon. Yes: push hers against the window, then his all the way against the wall. Let him come home and see her handiwork. She won't sleep with him again, not till Gabriel blows his trumpet.

She pictures her son in a girl's bedroom across town, shy but insistent, slipping inside something he doesn't understand but will pay for the rest of his life. Fifteen, same as her when she took up with Darryl. Here, back with the grown-ups, there are no touches, just words and longing glances across a fence. You could write a book about all the feeling trapped inside people's heads. She's the only one who picks something and sticks to it, even if she hates it, and goes where she's told. Doesn't look where she's not supposed to at a cookout, get led astray by movies or explosions in the sky. At the end of every party is punishment; any fool knows that.

Why does everyone else get to blur the lines?

When she looks up, sweating, she sees Diane standing in the doorway, staring at her, Bradford in her arms.

"Ronnie, you okay?"

The air tightens like a tuned string. Slow, with a sneer, Ronalda says, "Don't you got some poetry to read?"

Diane's blue eyes stare bad as Kenny's.

After a century of a moment, she lays Bradford on Darryl's bed. He wriggles there like a fat little worm. The two women watch him like he's the last thing they'll ever understand.

Diane leaves without a word, that sway in her hips, that tiny waist still there after three, grace she doesn't deserve.

There is no one here but Ronalda. That must be women's lib: go it alone because there's no one to trust. Just you and a choice of how many feet between the beds, a space where you can wave your arms like crazy, till you take off or fall to the floor.

ABOUT THE AUTHOR

Lyn Fairchild Hawks is the author of the novel, *How Wendy Redbird Dancing Survived the Dark Ages of Nought,* and other works forthcoming in the Girls Outside series. She is co-author of *The Compassionate Classroom: Lessons That Nurture Wisdom and Empathy* and *Teaching Romeo and Juliet: A Differentiated Approach.* She is also author of *Teaching Julius Caesar: A Differentiated Approach.* She is a member of True North Writers & Publishers. She lives with her family in Chapel Hill, North Carolina.

Contact Lyn at www.lynhawks.com

AWARDS

3.0
Finalist, 2010 NCSU Prize for Short Fiction, judged by Madison Smartt Bell
Finalist, 2008 Glimmer Train Family Matters contest
Retrograde
Finalist, 2008 Writers' Group of the Triad Contest, judged by Shannon Ravenel
The Flat and Weightless Tang-Filled Future
Winner of the Fall 2009 AROHO Orlando Short Fiction Prize